Also by K. E. Adamus

SUICIDES CLUB

a novella by

K. E. Adamus

based on a screenplay
"Suicides Club"
also written by
Katarzyna Adamus

2025
161 Days

Disclaimer

This book contains themes related to depression, suicidal thoughts, and emotional crisis.

Although the story is written in a dark-comedic tone, its purpose is *not* to trivialise or ridicule the subject of suicide. Rather, the intention is to raise awareness, open difficult conversations, and present the topic in a more accessible, human way.

If you are in crisis or feel like you're at the edge, please don't handle it alone.

Reach out to a mental health professional, a crisis line, a doctor, or anyone who can help.

You deserve support, and the world is not better without you in it.

On the day when Angela and Robert decided to commit suicide, the weather was astonishingly good.

It was a crisp winter day, with the sun overlooking the busy lives of Londoners.

Robert

Becky's pupils dilated at the sight of the ring, then suddenly narrowed.

Could it be that she was taking some kind of drugs?

The thought flashed through my mind. Nothing so far had indicated that. Becky trained hard to burn off the calories from the sweets she had a weakness for. A sportswoman would be unlikely to drug herself.

On the other hand, how many Olympic athletes have been disqualified for illegal substances found in their bodies?

I tried to push away the thought that this was taking too long.

The hard grey tiles installed in the kitchen at her special request pinched my knee. I knelt there, dressed in my best suit, holding out my hand with a ring worth four paychecks.

Becky remained silent. No emotion appeared on her face. She only looked down at me. And then she suddenly gasped for air and started yelling.

"In the kitchen? Did you just propose to me in the kitchen?"

"I'm still waiting for your answer," I replied quietly, not wanting to provoke her strange reactions.

I was also relieved that I hadn't chosen a crowded restaurant for the occasion. Becky was beautiful, with an "English rose" type of beauty, but she had an explosive personality. Any spark could cause ignition. She never disguised her words and sometimes said unpleasant things. I often wondered whether she actually thought of me in such a negative way, or whether she simply wanted to hurt me or win an argument.

Becky snatched the ring from my hand in one smooth motion and threw it into the sink. I gasped, my hand still outstretched.

Had the ring fallen into the drain pipe? Had my money just drained away with it, somewhere into the underworld of London?

I wanted so badly to check, to get out of this uncomfortable position. But I decided to keep my composure.

I lowered my hand.

"I see I didn't read your signals properly," I said.

That's when Becky exploded with anger. And I finally understood her point.

"After all, you *can* afford a trip to Paris! It's only a few hours by train! What do you expect me to post on my social media? '*Kitchen declarations*'?"

"As a creative interior decorator, you should have no trouble finding the right slogan," I replied.

Becky snorted with anger. This was bad. If my girlfriend couldn't articulate herself, it meant her anger had reached the extreme end of the spectrum. Almost like a 10 on the Beaufort scale.

She turned, losing her slipper, which amused me slightly.

A laugh burst out from the depths of my guts. I tried to restrain it — it was completely inappropriate for the situation — but whether it was embarrassment or some kitchen imp living there since Victorian times, I couldn't stop laughing.

Becky froze in the kitchen doorway. She looked at me like a praying mantis. The horror of her gaze made the laughter stick in my throat.

I coughed dryly, wanting to abruptly break the awkward silence. Finally, Becky spoke.

"I'm fed up with your sarcasm. You're like a robot! No romance, no feelings! Your parents were right!"

She rushed into the bedroom, yanked her suitcase from the wardrobe, opened all the drawers, and began stuffing her lingerie inside. I silently watched all these tiny trinkets, reminders of our intimate moments.

After the lingerie came the blouses. Becky was a minimalist, so she had a good chance of fitting all her clothes into one suitcase.

"As far as I know, my parents are against *you*, not me," I said.

Becky looked me straight in the eyes. She looked like a seagull swooping down to snatch someone's sandwich from their plate. Once again, I felt goosebumps.

Then she blurted out, "They offered me money to leave you."

"What?" I exclaimed.

"If they had offered more... But really, I know my price! You fit into your family well. No class!"

She snapped the suitcase shut, tossed her hair back, and looked at me with satisfaction.

She had won this battle.

Knocked out by these revelations, I slumped to the floor. I looked at Becky.

The beautiful blonde was gone. In her place, I saw the eyes of a psychopath.

Six years of my life flashed before me.

Becky shook her head in disgust, kicked off her slippers, quickly put on trainers, took a few quiet steps, and the wheels of her suitcase rattled away. The door slammed shut.

Six years. Six years of my life no longer counted. I had hesitated for a long time about whether Becky would be suitable material to be the mother of my children. After that praying-mantis–seagull gaze, I would be afraid to get closer to her than three metres.

My mind froze like an overtasked computer.

I got up and headed for the fridge; there were probably still some remnants of whiskey there.

Angela

Like many other souls, I was trapped in my office.

When the wall clock showed one o'clock, I carefully looked around and, not spotting any interest from my coworkers, I took the antidepressants out of my desk drawer.

Reaching for my mug of coffee, I almost suffocated as the tablet stuck in my throat—because I saw Shirley looking at me with pity in her eyes.

Shirley was almost a decade older, in her fifties, and to her, depression was simply "not wanting something badly enough." But this time she looked genuinely worried.

"You're on those antidepressants again? What happened with your dating life? You were starting to look so fresh, vivid, and happy." Shirley began her small investigation. "What happened?"

I quickly analysed the level of gossiping in Shirley's blood. She seemed focused on work and didn't usually share spicy details about others, so I decided to trust her.

"I'm still seeing him. It's going well. His name is Ahmed. But I'm scared something bad will happen. There are so many pretty, young girls around..."

"Oh no..." Shirley's compassion was like a balm on my itchy thoughts. I looked at her with gratitude.

But Shirley was looking over my head.

"Oh no... Michaela is coming here!" she finished.

Our boss, Michaela—looking like a sexier version of Marilyn Monroe—entered the office with the smell of extremely sweet, flowery perfume. Office gossip claimed that the perfume had been made specially for her, with extra pheromones, because Michaela finally wanted to find a husband instead of only organising weddings for others.

This time Michaela was smiling, and it was rare. No one knew how to behave or what was going to happen next.

I tried to search for something under the desk, desperate not to be the centre of attention for our psychopathic boss.

Unfortunately, Michaela was heading straight toward me. With news.

"Great job, Angela! This client is a perfect fit! A four-hundred-person wedding! Why didn't you tell us about him earlier?"

I remained on all fours under the desk and gave Michaela a confused look.

"What client?"

"Ahmed! He said you know each other well and asked for a 'friends and family discount.'"

Michaela, with a firm grip of her toned arm, grabbed my elbow, helped me up, and practically dragged me to the director's office.

And there he was. Ahmed. My date.

When he saw me, he laughed nervously. Next to him sat a beautiful woman in her thirties.

"Hi, Angela."

His voice was different from before. Gone was the softness and desire. He spoke to me as if I were his sister.

"What are you doing here? And who is she?"

I couldn't believe I had said something so awkward, but the words had already escaped.

"Angela, you are forgetting yourself," Michaela said coldly from behind me. "Ahmed and Aisha are committed to marrying and purchasing our best package."

"To marry? I had a date with this man yesterday!"

"Is that true?"

A glimpse of worry crossed the beautiful Aisha's face.

Ahmed's cheeks grew pale, and tiny drops of sweat appeared on his forehead.

"She's just a friend," he muttered.

"A friend with benefits!"

I couldn't believe it was the same man I had kissed yesterday. And the day before that. And...

"What?" Aisha looked equally confused.

"Don't listen to her. She's a bit crazy. She's seeing a therapist because of it. And look at her! She's fat! She's nothing compared to you!"

The lies poured from his mouth effortlessly.

I stared at them with wide-open eyes. I couldn't believe what was happening. Maybe I had overdosed on antidepressants and this was a hallucination?

No. This was the cruel reality.

Feeling the tears rising, I turned around and left the office, slamming the door.

I ran outside. I tried to light a cigarette, but my hands were shaking. Behind me, I heard Michaela's voice:

"We need to discuss your attitude. And these cigarette breaks! I made you responsible for this event. It will be good for your work ethic."

Robert

I was lying in bed, trying to fall asleep. I had had enough of everything. I couldn't even fucking fall asleep. I tried to come up with something to do, and then I felt the meaninglessness of my life. There was no point deceiving myself. It wouldn't get better. And as it was now, it wasn't good.

I grabbed Becky's pillow. Maybe the smell of her body and perfume would give me some semblance of feeling. Anything. Bitterness, regret, loneliness — whatever. But I felt only emptiness inside me, and this emptiness spread outward. It was as if the world had nothing more to offer.

The pillow smelled only of fabric softener. Apparently Becky had changed the sheets in the morning. I threw the pillow onto the floor.

Were all human relationships so one-sided, with only one person always caring about the relationship?

A wave of discouragement hit me. I didn't want to wake up in the morning, get up, go among people, and continue this whole charade.

Becky kept some pills in the drawer. Supposedly strong painkillers. I reached for them in the dark and pulled out a sachet. In the darkness, the package ominously mentioned a morphine derivative. The tablets were small and round — maybe so no one would get addicted too quickly?

It took me a few minutes to get them out. I opened the bottle of champagne standing nearby, waiting for our engagement night. I swallowed a handful of pills and washed them down with the alcohol.

The thought of saving my life crossed my mind. What a pathetic notion. I reached for the phone, but the thought of explaining myself to some NHS bureaucrat made me throw it as far from the bed as possible.

Surprisingly, I wasn't afraid. Maybe I was leaving too early, but nothing interesting was going to happen in my life anyway. Why cling to something that brings neither pleasure nor joy, when all that lies around the corner is the boredom of everyday life? I closed my eyes. For a moment, I felt a little sorry for my parents. But I wasn't going to suffer just to spare them distress.

Darkness suddenly enveloped me.

Angela

I was supposed to take my antidepressant an hour ago, yet here I am, lying down and feeling not only hopelessness but also shame. The whole company would know by tomorrow what happened. Michaela wouldn't let it go. God, how would I show my face to these people? And Shirley would definitely tell them how stupid I had been, describing Ahmed as a great guy.

And I really should take that damn pill. Or maybe... maybe take all of them? If there's no real life waiting on the other side, then why keep up this charade any longer?

Tomorrow would probably be cold and grey again, some crap would fall from the sky, and I still hadn't washed my clothes on time. I'd have to wear yesterday's outfit or put together something that didn't match at all. Plus, I was fat and unattractive. If only I could afford my own place. But no — I had to be under my parents' control. They decided what I ate and who visited us.

Fuck, I'd had enough. And there were only seven pills left. Maybe they'd do the job.

I swallowed them and washed down their bitter taste with water. I wanted to sleep for a few days. Maybe when I woke up... but did I even want to wake up? That was the question.

I looked out the window, listening to the sounds of the street. Maybe these people found some meaning in their daily hustle and bustle, but I'd had enough.

Sure, maybe I was weak. Everyone would think it was a broken heart. But it wasn't. It was a broken life. All those promises — it was supposed to be wonderful. Instead, it was just a series of humiliations, complaints, and boredom. Why keep it going?

Robert

I called Becky. A sob tore from my throat. I was cold despite the heater being on. Becky answered after twenty seconds.

"You were right! I was a loser! I couldn't even kill myself. Or your weird painkillers were too weak."

Silence fell on the other end of the line. Tears pushed their way out.

"Those were my birth control pills, you idiot. I didn't use painkillers."

"But they were in the package..."

I reached for the box and read aloud:

"Morphine derivative."

"I didn't want to get pregnant. Condoms are unreliable. Especially with you — I didn't want to get pregnant **with you**."

Emotions tore me apart. I cried and suddenly began to understand Becky's constant moods. It had to be because of those pills.

Everything could surely be fixed.

"How long did these emotions last? Now I understood your moods."

Sobs and a strange kind of sorrow choked my throat.

Let her come back, let her brew those weird shamanic teas.

"Please come back, I have to go to work."

I heard satisfaction in Becky's voice.

"No, we are over," she said — and I could swear she had smiled while saying it.

She was just a cold psychopath. How could I not have seen it?

Angela

I was awakened by a loud knocking on the door.

"Get up, it's already two in the afternoon," I heard my mother's voice.

Indeed. When I opened my eyes, it was bright outside. And I had been right about the weather. Maybe I had chosen the wrong profession and should have worked as a weather presenter?

No, definitely not with my looks.

I remembered yesterday's pills. What a shame they hadn't killed me.

Seriously, I didn't want to get up. I didn't want to keep pretending everything was fine. I covered my face with a blanket to block out the surrounding reality. A groan escaped me involuntarily.

Probably another organ would fail because of the overdose.

That was all I was going to get from this whole mess — just more suffering

Robert

Two toasts popped out of my retro-style toaster, which had always been my source of pride.

Pride? It always made underdone toast. It looked nice, but...

"I spent too many quids on you. I think I deserved well-done toast, didn't I?" I shouted at the blue machine.

The toaster remained indifferent to my internal turmoil. Becky had probably set it that way so the least-toasted pieces would contain fewer calories. Idiot. And I was an idiot too — for getting involved with her, and even just now begging her to come back.

I put the toasts back into the toaster and set the timer for a longer baking time.

Angela

I went to the kitchen, slightly staggering. Luckily, my parents had gone out somewhere.

I set the kettle to boil and threw slices of bread into the toaster. That red retro contraption got on my nerves. It burned the toast every time. This time, too, the slices came out dark brown.

I looked at the photograph with Ahmed, the one of us sitting on a park bench. It was our selfie — the one I had printed and put in a heart-shaped frame yesterday. It was supposed to be a gift for him.

I grabbed the toast, but it burned my fingers. I dropped it involuntarily, and it landed butter-side down on the photograph.

This was too much.

Did I really have to keep suffering?

And this damn toaster only ever burned the slices.

I definitely deserved something better.

I sat down on the floor. Tears flowed on their own.

I was already late for work, but maybe I would still make it to therapy. Maybe that idiot therapist would finally say something wise. For all the money she charged, she could at least put in some effort.

The only good thing about that therapy was that someone listened to me for a few dozen minutes. Although even she interrupted and criticised me, which made me cry at the end of each session. If only something wise would come out of her mouth for once.

Robert

Fortunately, my taxi-driver friend was free. Maybe I would at least make it to the therapy session. Marek pulled up in his black BMW. I sat next to him and suddenly started complaining, probably because of the female hormones coursing through my body.

"I'm telling you, that Iranian lunatic would cry again and take time away from my coaching hours. Take time? Steal it!" I began getting angry just at the thought of it.

"The fake blonde one?" Marek asked.

He knew a lot of stories from my life, so I navigated the conversation carefully to avoid him asking about Becky. I had no intention of breaking down in front of a guy.

"Yes, the champion of prolonged crying," I replied.

Marek gave me a furtive glance. We drove in silence for a few minutes; finally, he couldn't stand it anymore.

"I always wanted to ask... what kind of coaching makes people leave crying?"

I decided to be sincere. Let this topic intrigue him. Just don't talk about Becky.

"Actually, it is not coaching, it is psychotherapy. It's not that I am crazy and that's why I had to go. Although, to be honest, sometimes I fantasised about killing this woman. Maybe I don't have much sanity left."

Marek put both hands firmly on the steering wheel, so I quickly added:

"Now I only want to slap her — which, compared to killing, is actually an achievement."

Marek got lost in thought, then started talking about his business again. Seriously, he should have focused on driving better; he almost ran over an old lady who walked onto the street from behind a car.

But Marek just honked at her and launched into his tirade.

"I've already told you several times about my business idea. It might help more than a dozen therapists."

"Yes," I nodded politely. "You mentioned it. Express trips?"

Marek leaned back comfortably in his seat.

"Yes, express trips. Sometimes a bit demanding for the clients..."

"You should make it one day," I said as we were already approaching the office. "I'm not investing in risky start-ups, I told you already."

Marek slowed down to stop.

"You need that kind of challenge, and that's what I meant. I can organise something for you. Contact with nature is the best medicine."

"I'm too busy," I said, paying for the ride.

"Tell me about it. I actually have a second job right now. I'll be pretending — or rather, working — as a tour guide. The catch is, I forgot to read up on the history of Big Ben."

"Ah, you'll figure something out," I said as I got out. "If you don't know what to talk about, talk about the end of the world. That always grabs attention."

We laughed at my little joke.

Robert

A few minutes later, I no longer felt like laughing. I was pissed off. I caught myself rhythmically tapping a rolled-up newspaper against my knee. Great — soon I would start banging my head against the wall. A glance at my watch fuelled my frustration. This was taking too long.

I pulled a small notebook from my pocket titled *Crying Bitch*. I made a note of the additional minutes cut from my therapy session. There were several pages of these entries. It dawned on me how much I had been disregarded. I had had enough.

The door opened, and the bleached-blonde Iranian woman came out. As usual, she was sobbing and loudly blowing her nose.

The psychotherapist peeked out from behind the door. She had grey, uncoloured hair and probably only practised yoga asanas outside of work. I was about to shatter her calm.

Or maybe it was better not to mess with the therapist? She knew all my secrets. But when she smiled and said, "I'm sorry, we just had some..." — I had had enough.

"Same shit each week!" I shouted. "She should book two hours in a row!"

The therapist smiled indulgently and started some stupid lecture.

"There is a concept of a cup..."

That was too much. She was about to start talking about a half-empty or half-full glass. Cold bitch. There were only twenty-five minutes left of my session, and she was going on about a glass.

"I'm a fuckin' realist!" I continued shouting. "She should book two or three hours for her crying. Plus, she has never apologised!"

The therapist smiled calmly. She probably felt her power. We came here to talk about our problems, we paid for it, and she couldn't care less about those problems.

"That's another theory," she began. "Let's use the example of a bottle. Her bottle of worries and problems is full. A few more drops and it will overflow..."

"My bottle is a fizzy drink and it just exploded," I replied. Someone should save this pathetic lady. But not with my money. I would find another therapist — one who focused fairly on all patients. I was not going to pay for her handkerchiefs.

I headed towards the door. Emotions were boiling inside me, probably still because of the female hormones.

"You will come back. Everyone comes back to me," the therapist said, unmoved, still smiling.

"First they had to leave you, right? Everyone probably leaves — except that blonde lunatic."

"Did you buy the book I was telling you about?" she asked.

I didn't reply and walked out.

Outside, bitterness boiled inside me. A few billion — or trillion — people in this world, and there was no one to talk to about your problems, not even for money. What the hell was going on in this vale of tears?

The psychotherapist leaned out the window and shouted at the top of her lungs:

"The book's title is *I Don't Want to Die!*"

Fantastic. Now everyone would know the darkness that enveloped my soul and mind, all because this wretch couldn't keep her mouth shut.

"Confidentiality! You're so damn professional! Everyone in this area could hear you!" I shouted back.

Marek was at his second job. I had no desire to squeeze into the metro, bus, or ride with some random taxi driver. I opened an app on my phone and decided to walk to work instead. Maybe some fresh air would work its so-praised-by-everyone wonders.

Robert

A few meters ahead, I saw a bookstore. And inside, the blonde occupier of my therapy hours was browsing among the shelves. Maybe it was time for a confrontation. Why should I have endured all the kicks from fate and people in silence, watching how far they would go? Time to put an end to this. And who better to practise my first confrontation on than someone who truly deserved it?

I walked into the bookstore.

The bottle-blonde was trying to reach some hefty tome on the top shelf. She was clearly too short for the task. I walked over, ready to unload my grievances on her. First, I glanced at the shelf. Up there stood what appeared to be the last, lonely copy of the book recommended by our therapist.

So, she wanted to kill herself too? Time to make that decision easier for her.

I grabbed the book effortlessly.

The blonde reached out for it.

"Thank you."

"You're welcome," I replied, walking away with the book toward the checkout.

She caught up with me a moment later, probably frozen in shock back there for a bit.

"That's *my* book! I saw it first!" she yelled.

"Looks like nature was against you on this occasion. The laws of nature are sometimes brutal," I replied, looking down at her.

"You don't understand, I really *need* that book!"

"You'll now have an extra hour with our shrink. It should compensate. I quit today — had enough of your melodrama!"

"Shrink? Do you mean Mrs. Smith? How do you know I go to her? Are you *stalking* me?"

"For your information, you're too plump for me. I was the next patient in line. You owe me this book for countless dozens of missed full hours..."

My voice caught in my throat. I silently bought the book.

The blonde stared at me in disbelief. Suddenly, she grabbed a hefty tome of *Emotional Intelligence* and threw it at me.

I ducked, mildly amused. The book landed on a stack of bestsellers, wreaking havoc. Mangled books crashed to the floor. She would pay for this—no doubt the bill would be hefty.

Satisfied, I walked outside, but of course my euphoria lasted all of a millisecond. Because why would it be any other way?

I could still hear the blonde's voice calling me a jerk from inside the bookstore.

But I was already focusing on two brutes jumping out of a van parked by the sidewalk. They didn't look friendly, and it was clear they were interested in me.

I wasn't mistaken. They grabbed me by the arms and unceremoniously shoved me into the van, which screeched off with a sharp burst forward.

I caught a glimpse of the blonde running out of the bookstore, surprised not to see my miserable self anywhere. At least there was that tiny bit of satisfaction from this whole mess.

Angela

I was chatting with Shirley over coffee. Of course, I wasn't telling her the whole truth. That would hopefully remain between me, the bookstore clerk, and the handsome, understanding policeman who had been called to the scene.

"...and then he just bought *my* book, lecturing me about the laws of nature! I wanted to hit him with a copy of *Emotional Intelligence*—it was big enough to wipe that stupid grin off his face. But it wasn't in my nature... he was probably right..." I rambled awkwardly.

"Why don't you just order the book online?" Shirley asked.

As if it were that simple.

"My mom is really nosy. She opens all my parcels," I admitted, embarrassed.

"Oh no," Shirley said in a familiar tone.

That was when Michaela entered our office.

"This is your big opportunity to let go of your ego. Mr. Ahmed and his fiancée are here. Please apologize to them for your previous behaviour," she said loudly, addressing me.

Ahmed and Aisha were sitting in Michaela's office, holding hands. Forget the guy—what mattered most right now was keeping my job. This was going to be quite a lesson in humility, though Michaela had no idea how big of one.

I turned to his fiancée.

"I wanted to apologise for my past behaviour," I said quietly. "I didn't have my contact lenses in and probably mistook your fiancé for someone else."

I saw an unhealthy satisfaction on her face. She was enjoying my humiliation. I wondered if she believed him or me—or simply chose whichever version suited her best.

"Probably? You're still not sure? You said you were sleeping with this man. And now you can't recognise him?" She mocked me.

Of course. She didn't care about the truth—she was probably only interested in Ahmed's shares in his father's companies. Poor thing. She'd be in for a surprise when she saw the prenup.

She laughed at me out loud.

"Sometimes you don't know the real face of a lover..." I said enigmatically.

"Ladies, let's focus on our marriage ceremony," Ahmed interrupted quickly.

"I'm not sure I want her to work on our wedding event..." Aisha began complaining, trying to worsen my situation in Michaela's eyes.

"I have an amazing colleague here who will make sure your wedding is a five-star event," I said, deciding to use this opportunity to get out of organising the reception for this guy. Just five days ago, he had been promising to cook my favourite meals for me for the rest of his life.

But Aisha wasn't about to let me off the hook.

"Actually, I've changed my mind. You know our culture well. I'm sure we'll cooperate wonderfully," she said, then started giggling like the idiot she most likely was.

Serves him right.

Involuntarily, I joined in her laughter.

Let him suffer with this shrew for the rest of his life.

Robert

The van seemed to have stopped in some secluded place—judging by the lack of street noise.

The kidnappers were arguing about whose balaclava belonged to whom. Eventually, they seemed to reach a consensus. They yanked the sack off my head.

"Today, we're quite friendly..." said the fatter one.

"Yes, indeed..." I began, but the other kidnapper's fist slamming into my stomach knocked the breath out of me for a moment.

"You're not allowed to talk. Is that clear?" said the fatter one.

Another punch to my stomach. I nodded to show I understood.

Who were these idiots? Why had they kidnapped me?

Did I resemble someone they were after?

They would be in for a surprise. But that only made it worse for me—they would probably kill me right away.

"You made a false estimation of our company expenses. But you'll fix it at your daily meeting this afternoon, right?"

So it *was* about me, after all. Damn it.

Or maybe they had made a mistake?

"I'm not your accountant! I work for a fraud investigation company!" I shouted.

Another punch to the stomach.

"As I said, today we're friendly. But we're moody. Who knows what might happen tomorrow? Now, take off all your clothes."

"What?"

From Marek's later account, I learned how ridiculous the whole situation had looked from his perspective.

He had been standing, surrounded by a group of nuns, trying to piece together a coherent story about Big Ben.

"As you see behind me, this is one of the most famous landmarks in London. It is, like, very famous. I didn't study its history, but I can tell you a very interesting legend about it. If the clock, let's say, stops, our world will be, let's say, in real trouble. But everything is in order and working well, under British care."

Then Big Ben's clock had begun chiming 4 P.M., and suddenly it jammed while counting the third strike.

At the same time, I was thrown out in the middle of Westminster Bridge.

The nuns were just witnessing the clock's malfunction.

"You have nothing to worry about, in this country almost everything goes smoothly..." Marek had been reassuring them.

And that was when I ran down the stairs straight into their group.

"Did I mention the word *almost*?" Marek added later, planning to call me to find out how I had ended up there — and in Adam's attire.

Without paying attention to him, I ran away.

The nuns giggled like teenagers and probably took hundreds of photos of me.

"Could you show a little mercy, sisters?" I said, turning around and exposing my bare ass to them as I retreated under the bridge.

I planned to hide there and ask someone for help — a phone or some clothes.

However, passersby treated me like air.

A homeless couple watched the scene. They were sitting close together and seemed to be having a great laugh.

Finally, the homeless man shouted at me.

"Hey, you OK?"

"No, not really," I answered, with the last bit of pride left in my voice.

"What happened to you, mate? Is it some vegans' protest march?" his woman asked.

"I am a pescatarian," I replied, catching myself on the absurdity of the statement. I was standing naked in the city centre and advocating for eating fish. Wonderful.

"I thought Jehovah's Witnesses were weird, but it looks like I didn't know pesca... pesca..."

"Pescatarian!" I shouted.

"...that time..." the homeless woman finished the sentence.

"My name is George, and this is Alice," he introduced them both.

"Do you have any spare clothes, please?" I asked, ignoring the pleasantries.

"We might have some, if you do us a favour."

"I'll pay you later, if that's okay?" I offered.

"It's not about the money! Not everything is about the money, man," George replied.

Robert

A few minutes later, having struck a deal that was clearly not in my favour and feeling as though I had signed a pact with the devil, I sprinted into Westminster station dressed in dirty tracksuit bottoms, a women's T-shirt, and barefoot. The homeless couple hadn't lent me any money. I now looked just like one of them, so without engaging in unnecessary discussions, I vaulted over the ticket barrier and dashed toward the platforms.

"Stop!"

The station staff—usually nowhere to be found—suddenly appeared in a sizable group and started chasing me. One of them was probably a former track athlete, because he caught up with me in seconds despite my considerable head start.

He grabbed me by the shirt. I threw a light punch and managed to break free. The sound of tearing fabric was drowned out by the departure signal of the District Line train.

I jumped on at the last second.

Robert

And there I was, in the building of my company.

Almost at my goal, debating whether to listen to my kidnappers or report them.

But first, I needed to get past the gates guarded by the security officer.

And here was the problem:

The jerk was pretending he didn't know me.

"I pass this gate every working day before 8 a.m. Don't tell me you don't know me!" I shouted, irritated.

"I don't recall you, indeed," he replied calmly. He was savouring his moment of power.

"I have a very important meeting on the top floor. Without me, we might lose—"

"If the meeting is that important, it's in my best business not to interrupt it. Sorry," the guard answered coolly. He wouldn't call, and he certainly wouldn't let me inside.

I started losing my patience and yelled at him:

"You don't understand! I've been working on this case all year. A whole fucking year taken out of my life!"

"Maybe it's time to rest. Outside, if possible. Don't take it personally; if you really work in this building, you should be aware of high-security rules," the jerk mocked me further. And to think, I had thought he was a decent guy.

I decided to ignore him. I walked through the gate and headed toward the elevator.

The bastard was stronger than he looked—he dragged me out of the building.

As I left, he added:

"Maybe if you had said 'Good morning' at least once, then I would remember you."

Oh, I would give him a *good morning*—just you wait.

Robert

I stood on a nearby bridge, gazing down at the murky waters of the Thames. Below me was a safety net, designed to give a second chance to those who might try to jump.

"They don't make it easy for suicides now. All these nets. It's not that easy to kill yourself, at least here," I heard a friendly voice say. A young guy in a suit had stopped next to me, contemplating the net below.

"Are you suggesting I should go and kill myself somewhere else?" I snapped, trying to get him to leave me alone. But this guy was odd—he just stood there and kept talking.

"Yeah, something like this."

"You could show some empathy!" I retorted angrily. I was freezing, miserable, and completely fed up, and this guy, instead of encouraging me to keep living, was practically suggesting I kill myself. And on top of that, he just kept rambling like a lunatic.

"We try not to make it emotional. It can break deals," he said.

"'We'? You mean who? And what deals? Do I look like I'm in the mood for some business chat?"

Then he pulled a leaflet out of his pocket and pressed it into my numb hand.

"Whenever you're ready, man. I've got to go. We're understaffed this season."

He walked off, continuing across the bridge. I looked at the leaflet. There was a logo and title — *Suicides Club* — an address, phone number, and a tagline:

"Save your life for Christmas."

That was it.

I tossed the paper into the river.

Lunatics were everywhere, honestly — but in London, they clearly hadn't caught them all yet.

Robert

Some time later, I decided to head home. Near Embankment Station, I walked past two police officers with my head down. They suddenly perked up at the sight of me. I started running, which, of course, they took as an invitation to chase me.

I darted into one street, then another. Suddenly, I spotted the logo from the leaflet — *Suicides Club*. Behind me, the sounds of pursuit grew louder — whistles and shouts. Thankfully, UK police were unarmed; otherwise, instead of whistles, there would probably have been gunshots. Though really, why shoot at a homeless guy?

Despite my rational musings, I decided to hide. I slipped into the Suicides Club. Let's see what kind of crowd this was.

Turns out, it was quite the peculiar one.

As I closed the door behind me to avoid making it too easy for the police to find me, I was enveloped in sudden darkness.

"Just follow the light at the end of the corridor," a voice called out from somewhere ahead.

"You've got to be kidding me," I muttered. Once my eyes adjusted, I did indeed see a faint glow in the distance.

I headed toward it. The light seeped out from under a door.

I pushed it open, and before me was what looked like an old ballet rehearsal room.

In the middle, there was a circle of five chairs. An elderly man of African descent sat in one of them. Next to him, unsurprisingly, was the

25

blonde from therapy, then an empty chair, and two teenagers — a boy and a girl — who looked like they were part of a rock band.

The old man looked like he was in charge of this bizarre gathering.

"Please, take a seat," he said in a calm voice.

Robert

God, I thought, *maybe I am not ready to die after all if it means ending up with this lot of lunatics.*

"I'm just here for a minute," I said loudly.

"Then please sit down and don't interrupt," the man responded.

I sat next to the blonde. What was her name? I thought the therapist had called her Angela. She didn't seem to recognise me, so I decided to annoy her. I inhaled deeply.

"Nice perfume. Will you still be able to afford it after paying your bookstore bill?"

"Nice clothes," she replied. "Looks like I'm doing better than you."

The leader of the group insisted on being called Coach—*oh God*—and began the meeting.

"I think we are all present now. Let me introduce our club rules," Coach began. "Your goal, all of you, was to end your miserable lives. But we understand that things might not have gone as planned. Maybe it was the wrong pills. Maybe not enough of them. Whatever the case, we are here to help you finish the job before Christmas. No more suffering, no more problems. But it will cost you a little money. Specifically, £100,000."

The teenager in the chair next to me started getting agitated. I didn't blame him.

"What? I thought you wanted to help us live happy lives? Who the fuck are you?"

"We need to screen all potential members first," Coach replied calmly, "then we'll provide the necessary information."

What the hell had I stumbled into? Maybe I was hallucinating from stress or something.

"I don't have that kind of money!" the teenager snapped.

I couldn't blame him.

"Neither do I. I'm broke," said the girl.

"Then please come back in a few years," Coach said matter-of-factly.

I must have misheard him. The room fell silent.

"What kind of charity is this? And that tagline—'Save your life before Christmas!'—what the fuck?" the teenager exclaimed, looking around. My outfit clearly didn't inspire trust, and Angela probably didn't either.

"A good advertisement leverages business," Coach responded serenely.

"All charities are bullshit. They just steal money... and businessmen are even worse!" the girl chimed in.

Both teenagers stormed out, slamming the door behind them.

I couldn't afford to follow their lead—there were still whistles echoing outside. Besides, this bizarre situation was too intriguing to pass up. And then there was Angela—whatever her role in this mess was.

"And what about you?" Coach turned to us. "Are you ready for such a commitment? Then listen to our rules. The introductory rule is as follows: you can still change your mind. The next meeting is in two days. If you come back, it means you're signing the agreement. We're against paperwork, but showing up to the next meeting means you're committed. The meeting is over."

Robert & Angela

I followed Angela out, glancing around for the police. I also decided to irritate the blonde.

"Are you coming back here?" I asked very politely.

"None of your business!"

"I just wanted to borrow a tenner. But if you're not coming back..." I replied.

"I've met many assholes in my life, but honestly, you could train them."

Angela looked annoyed. And it was probably not just because of me—I wasn't about to flatter myself. She was probably telling the truth about the jerks in her life, but why should I have cared? If she hadn't been stealing time from my therapy sessions, maybe I wouldn't have been in the situation I was in now.

"You owe me money for all the time you stole from my therapy hours. I had a notebook with the calculations..." I said coldly.

"A long walk might do you good. Maybe you'll remember the exact amount of my 'debt,'" Angela snapped back, then turned and headed toward a bus stop.

I walked in the opposite direction. From time to time, I asked people for spare change, but they ignored me completely. Ah yes—Christmas was definitely coming.

Robert

Outside my home, the homeless couple who had lent me clothes was sitting there.

This didn't bode well.

"Sorry, guys, I can't invite you in. I have trust issues with strangers," I said, just in case they tried to invite themselves inside. But no, they didn't want to come in.

"We have trust issues too. We were just checking if you gave us the correct address. You might not care, but it's a matter of life and death for us. We'll come back in a few days to see if any post arrives. By the way, do you have any spare clothes for an interview?" George asked.

I nodded. He said he would come by for the clothes.

I went inside, filled the bathtub with hot water, and looked at what was left of my feet after walking barefoot on London's cold pavements. I thought about the women in my life and started swearing under my breath.

This was definitely their fault.

Robert

I was sitting at work, staring blankly at the screen. Nothing registered through my senses, but I had to focus on the numbers. It was a nightmare.

The boss burst in, as usual without knocking. And, of course, he was shouting.

"Are you on their payroll? How much of a bribe did they offer you?"

"Excuse me?"

Genuine astonishment coloured my voice. We had known each other for years—what kind of nonsense was he accusing me of?

"Why didn't you come to the meeting?"

"I was kidnapped. They left me without clothes, without a phone. Ask that bastard downstairs! The damn security guy didn't let me into the building!" I began to vent.

"Are you on any drugs?"

Clearly, my story didn't sound credible.

"No."

"Then you won't mind a quick finger prick test?"

"I might be on female contraception pills. Don't ask about it, please," I said quietly, though with the door wide open, several pairs of ears had probably already overheard.

"I thought I had good judgment about people—until now. I'll send you an official meeting invitation. We'll also need to conduct a fraud check on your accounts."

The boss looked deeply unhappy. Not that I could blame him.

He finally left, and silence fell.

Just in case, I logged into my account. Maybe the kidnappers had planted something there?

But no—the only thing missing was money.

A £2,000 transaction labelled **"Christmas Time."**

Angela

Finally, it was lunch break—which we still spent in the office, because Michaela's greed had made her choose an office location far from civilization. As a result, there was nowhere to grab coffee and gossip about that beautiful monstrosity.

But that wasn't what was bothering me today.

Someone had had the audacity to brazenly steal money from my account—the money I'd saved for a vacation trip. I hadn't decided where to go yet, but surely somewhere beautiful, a place whose atmosphere could chase away my melancholy.

I called the bank.

The customer service lady—or rather, the witch from customer service—didn't care at all that my money had vanished.

"It must be a mistake! I don't celebrate Christmas!" I exclaimed indignantly when she tried to tell me that I must have donated the money to charity.

"Please contact the organization," she droned in a monotone.

"What do you mean, I should contact the creditor? Tell me first, who is it? Santa Claus? He's supposed to *give* money, not steal it from bank accounts!"

Then I heard the address of the Suicides Club branch.

Damn. How was I supposed to get myself out of this scene now?

"Thank you for the address. Yes, I'll check it," I murmured into the phone before quickly hanging up.

Shirley, munching her usual stinky cheese-and-onion sandwich, watched me closely.

"Did you find out who it was? It's a lot of money!"

I knew she was worried, but it was better to change the subject.

"I'll sort it out. I have bigger problems. That Iranian couple—I just can't deal with them anymore..."

Shirley took the bait. For the next several minutes, I listened to a lecture about how "out of sight, out of mind," how women didn't need to start families, and how nature was weird because women ought to be physically stronger than men, given they had stronger nerves and psyches.

During a brief pause, I interjected that most women were far from rational during their periods. Unfortunately, this earned me a tirade about the wonders of menopause.

I had never suspected Shirley of being such a feminist, so I glanced at her reflection in the office wardrobe.

Yep, she was wearing a bra—probably even a push-up.

Feeling reassured, I sipped my coffee and strategised about how to get my money back from those nutcases at the Suicides Club. I nodded occasionally, pretending to listen to Shirley's monologue. Sometimes, that was all talkers needed—just to vent, not to have a conversation.

Angela & Robert

Right after finishing work, without dinner, and after multiple metro transfers, I arrived at the headquarters of the Suicides Club.

I walked straight into the middle of an argument.

"I will make a proper investigation of your accounts! And maybe you know or not, but if you had used a cheap calculator, you will be fucked!"

Robert's yelling was audible even from the corridor.

When I entered the room, Robert was pacing back and forth by the window, completely ignored by Coach, who was calmly marking something in a newspaper.

"Explain this to me properly. I use a free online calculator," he finally responded, putting the newspaper down.

"Ha! Even good calculators give different results each time, especially with complex calculations. And believe me, these few pounds here and there, yes, it makes a difference for HMRC!"

Robert triumphantly pointed a finger at Coach.

"It looks like you were robbed, but instead of getting your money back, you prefer to prove that you have a better calculator," I said to Robert, who immediately fell silent.

"He might not care, but how could you steal money from me? What kind of charity is this?" I asked Coach. I felt like I was begging for someone else's money, even though it was my own, earned under that wretched Michaela.

Coach looked at us and gestured toward the chairs. I sat down, exhausted from the long journey.

Robert leaned against the windowsill. Maybe he could afford to keep his pride?

I couldn't.

"We are a charity for ex-hitmen and their families. We just had to run an accounts check to see if you could afford our fees. Anyway, since you are here, you are now obliged to follow our rules."

"I wouldn't have come if you hadn't stolen my money!"

My raised voice probably echoed for several streets around.

"You could call the police; that would be a more natural reaction, given that you have our address."

Coach remained unfazed. And he was right.

But what would I even have told them? That I wanted to kill myself? They'd put me in a hospital for observation, and then my parents, friends, and colleagues would all find out. I'd be labelled a lunatic for the rest of my life.

So I fell silent.

Robert also said nothing from his perch on the windowsill.

Coach turned to him.

"Maybe we will have a chance to talk about calculations on another occasion."

He began folding up the newspaper. Of course—what had he been marking?

The obituaries. Most likely his charity's handiwork.

"Now, both of you, please sit down comfortably and listen carefully. At the last meeting, I didn't tell you the full set of rules. That was just an introductory session. You didn't listen to me then—well, that was your mistake. Or maybe those were subconscious choices. If I were in your place, I'd be all ears now."

Robert & Angela

Coach had started talking about something, but very quietly. So I sat down with them. If someone had walked in, they would probably have thought it was some kind of group therapy. I pushed away intrusive thoughts and focused on what Coach was saying.

"I will start with a small task."

Coach got up and handed us mirrors.

"What do you see when you look at yourself in the mirror?" he asked.

"It's a bit personal, don't you think?"

Angela clearly had objections about sharing. Given her weight, I wasn't surprised. She probably had complexes.

"Your life is in my hands. Nothing is personal now," Coach replied.

I stared at my face reflected in the mirror.

"I see a middle-aged man, cheated by life," I said.

"How deep..." Angela commented sarcastically on my statement.

That was too much. For a moment, I wanted to kill her — and for free, unlike Coach. She would have left money in her account for some heirs.

"You did not give me a chance to use my psychotherapy time, so bog on..."

Coach turned to Angela.

"Your turn."

Angela took a deep breath.

"I see fading youth and beauty..."

I couldn't hold back and started laughing.

"As if you have ever been beautiful! Ha, ha, ha!"

"I'm not surprised that life cheated on you. Maybe if you were more handsome, it wouldn't focus on someone else," Angela retorted.

I stopped laughing. We locked eyes, but Coach interrupted with his speech.

"There is no coincidence in the universe. Everything happens for a reason. That's why the first rule is that you will be working on your assignments together. You've met here for some reason, probably to learn something from each other," he began.

"Working? You are going to rob us for a hilarious amount of money, then kill us, but before... you expect us to do work for you?" I asked mockingly.

"I must agree this time. It doesn't sound good to me."

Angela also didn't like the idea.

"Let me explain a few things. Firstly, I suspect that you two are destined to be together."

Coach smiled at us. Damn — where had I ended up? This guy was a lunatic.

"Oh my God! Why did you imprint this in my innocent mind? I can't unsee what I saw now," I said out loud, because the vision of Angela in a wedding dress would probably haunt me in nightmares.

"What have you seen?" Coach asked.

"I saw her naked!"

I decided to dramatize the situation. Everything was already absurd enough.

"How dare you! You won't see me naked in a million years," Angela's outrage seemed sincere.

"I doubt you will live that long. Anyway, I agree with you that it's not a good idea."

"Looks like you've already given a thought or two to the idea of being together," Coach smirked mischievously.

A shiver ran down my spine, and suddenly I felt cold.

"A lie repeated often enough becomes reality. So stop talking about it, please. I'm more curious about the rules than about planning a wedding with this madwoman here," I said.

"You're madder. I saw you buying that book in the bookstore."

"Do you mean the book you were after, or are you losing your senses? I haven't been to a bookstore in ages."

"That's why you're so stupid!"

Coach interrupted our argument.

"Rule number two... Very important!"

He paused for a moment.

"We can't take your lives until we are 100% sure that you have lived them fully and understood the value of life. That's why we will assign you a few tasks. You will work as partners here."

"With this jerk?" Angela asked.

"Please choose a charity of your choice for your partner. He must spend five hours volunteering."

"I think a dementia care home would be a good place for him. He likes to read, so, for example, reading to the patients should be easy for him and blissful for the elderly..."

Angela had no trouble choosing a place for me.

"Great. Now your turn, Robert."

I thought for a moment about how to get back at this lunatic.

"I think working with the homeless might be a very good experience for this fluffy lady."

"Fluffy? Not everyone likes to be as skinny as you are. Your calves, for example, are so thin that I'm surprised you can walk."

Of course, I had hit a sore spot.

"You must have great balance on yours!" I snapped back immediately.

"That's enough!"

Apparently, we had pissed off Coach.

"Get out! I did not finish with the rules. Now you will be in the darkness with your rules awareness. Thanks for your courtesy."

"When is the next meeting?" Angela asked.

"You have one week. Whoever screws up their volunteering time will be out of the program immediately. You have to volunteer in one go for five hours. Five hours sharp! Goodbye!"

Robert

Slightly stunned by Coach's speech, I stepped outside. Angela was walking rather energetically ahead of me. It was actually *my* walking pace—otherwise, I would have overtaken her a while ago. So I followed about a meter behind. Apparently, she was headed to the same bus stop as me.

Suddenly, she turned around and smacked me on the left shoulder with her handbag. Clearly, something had pissed her off again. But at least she wasn't crying.

"Stop following me!" she yelled and hit me with the bag again, this time with force.

What did she carry in that thing? It actually hurt a little.

"I'm going in the same direction," I replied. "What did you think—that I fell in love with you?"

Another hit, and now I was getting annoyed too. And it wasn't easy to get me mad. This woman clearly had a talent for it.

"Oh my God! The queen of the pavement!" I yelled. "Does it belong only to you? I'm so sorry, madam. By the way, will you marry me?" I added sarcastically.

"Go somewhere else, you freak!"

I overtook this lunatic. Now *she* was the one following me.

"Okay, I'll go. But stop fantasizing about me," I tossed over my shoulder.

We kept walking at the same pace. I decided to get my revenge for the handbag attacks.

"Stop following me!" I shouted. "And stop watching my ass!"

"This skinny ass?" Angela retorted scornfully.

"So you *were* watching it?"

This woman definitely deserved my revenge.

So this time I shouted loud enough for everyone at the bus stop we were approaching to hear:

"Help! I'm being followed by an ass-watcher! Help!"

I had to flee, because surprisingly, Angela could run fast.

She started to chase me, but I was quicker. I jumped onto the bus. The doors slammed shut in Angela's face.

I waved at her.

She was furious, and only after a moment did she realise that everyone was staring at her with a mix of disgust and curiosity. A female pervert, in broad daylight, chasing a skinny Jew? Things like this didn't even happen often in London. Her exotic looks only added spice to the entire scene.

Angela

I still had a bit of time. The food bank didn't open for another several minutes. And to top it off, it was raining. I was wearing old jeans, stylishly distressed, and a khaki jacket. I had a backpack too—just in case some homeless guy decided to snatch my handbag. I was going to cover my head with a newspaper and hoped I wouldn't get so soaked that I caught pneumonia and died in the most ridiculous way possible—as a volunteer in London. Taking my own life would have been much more romantic.

In the shop, I tried to make small talk with the shopkeeper. He was Kurdish, so I didn't exactly spark his sympathy.

"I heard there's a food bank nearby?"

"You bought the wrong newspaper!" he replied, without a shred of logic in his answer.

"Wrong newspaper?" I repeated, confused.

"Yes. Local job adverts are in this one." He pointed to the local paper. "You think who is paying for your food bank? Me! It's from my taxes. Get your lazy ass to work!"

I threw a twenty-pound note onto the counter and grabbed a copy of *The Economist*.

The Kurd still glared at me with hostility, so without waiting for my change, I left and slammed the door behind me.

Outside, it was raining even harder.

I found the food bank on my own. With the newspaper still covering my head from the downpour, I approached a queue of homeless people waiting by the canteen. I walked straight to the entrance.

"Hey! The queue! We don't know where you're from, but if you live here, you should respect the line," one of the homeless men shouted.

Surprised, but still agitated from the incident in the shop, I asked politely, although my nerves were starting to fray.

"Pardon?"

"And you should learn our language too!" another homeless man commented.

The others in the queue nodded their heads in agreement.

"I'm a volunteer!" I tried to explain.

"You look more like our competition, not a volunteer, lady. Volunteers are way, way better kept."

That was too much. I had come here to spend one of the last hours of my life serving soup, and all that was waiting for me here was another serving of contempt. Enough!

"I took off my jewelry so you wouldn't steal it. Happy now?" I exploded.

All the homeless people fell silent. I moved toward the door without any further interruption and entered the building.

Robert

I managed to convince the nurses that their patients needed someone to read them books.

At first, they looked at each other and burst out laughing.

My further arguments about the moral and ethical importance of such a gesture only made them laugh harder.

"Help, help! Nurse, help!" came an elderly cry from one of the rooms.

"Let's put him with Greg, maybe we'll get a moment of peace," one of them said.

To my surprise, she led me straight to the room where the call for help was coming from.

Greg, an old Englishman, close to a hundred years old, was lying in his bed, cutting diamond shapes out of his blanket with nail scissors.

"What the fuck? Where did you get the scissors? And what do you think you're doing today, Greg?"

The nurse clearly didn't approve of Greg's activity.

"Help, help!" the old man began to shout.

"Stop shouting. What do you think you're doing today?" the nurse repeated her question.

"I'm going to die. I'm just preparing food for my funeral. I'll cook it later..."

Greg was clearly a difficult case.

Her words confirmed my suspicions.

"He's one of the worst cases. We're actually grateful for your time. I doubt he'll listen to your reading, but at least you'll keep an eye on him for a few hours, right?"

"Help, help! Call the nurse! I'm gonna die! Help! Help!"

Greg clearly didn't like having his scissors taken away.

The nurse sighed and left the room.

I sat down next to the bed. Greg fixed a stubborn stare on me.

"I'm not your son or anyone from the family," I decided to open the conversation.

"That's for sure. You're too skinny. By the way, that's a weird way to introduce yourself. Do you think I'm dumb?"

"I brought a few books. Would you like me to read to you?"

"I can read myself!"

The old man was clearly not in the mood. "What are you after? My money? It's all going to orphans. Well, some of them..."

"Really? You don't have a family?"

"Ha! So they did send you! I knew it. They're not getting a single penny. The will is the will."

It was getting interesting. Either I had been nosy, or I had wanted to convince myself that others had it worse than I did—and that was why I started probing into his private tragedy.

"I don't know your family, but why are you so angry at them?"

"I'm doing them a favor. They have to stand on their own feet, not wait around for my money. It'll all go to education grants for orphans."

"I see."

"Now, get the hell out of here and call one of the nurses."

"I can't," I replied.

Angela

I approached someone who looked like the organizer of this whole circus. The homeless people came in with me and started shouting over each other, ignoring the food.

"What's going on here?" the organizer asked in confusion. "George, maybe you can explain this to me?"

"Okay, people, I'll tell him about it," said the man who didn't like my outfit choice for the occasion, finally quieting everyone down.

Silence fell.

"This lady doesn't care about us. She probably just wants a nice-looking 'volunteer job' on her CV," George began his speech. "What do you think, Peter?" he turned to the organizer.

Peter, stuttering slightly, responded after a brief pause.

"We can't choose our volunteers. It's a rough area. I'm glad she showed up and that we have an extra pair of hands to work with. You don't have to like her. But you can try to educate her. She'll be here for the next few hours."

The homeless people looked at me and Peter in silence at first. Then they gathered into small groups and started chatting amongst themselves.

It looked like a new conspiracy theory had just found a fresh, bubbling spring.

I didn't like the way they kept glancing at me or the fingers pointing discreetly at my ten-year-old sneakers.

"I knew it would be hard, but this is more hostile than I was expecting," I sighed.

"You'll be working here, handing out food," Peter replied, completely ignoring my comment.

"Can I help in the kitchen instead?"

"All is done there. But don't worry, it'll take no more than two hours. After the meal, you'll just wash the dishes."

Two hours? According to Coach's instructions, I was supposed to work five hours straight. Who knew what that weirdo would do if he found out I hadn't followed through? If he had access to my bank account data, he could easily find out where I lived and worked. I had definitely stepped into something seriously messy.

"I have five hours of my time today," I offered to Peter.

"What are you after? On a CV, you don't have to be specific about volunteer hours."

He looked at me like I'd just killed his favorite cat with a pancake.

"It's more of a betting issue," I said quietly.

"So you've got a gambling problem! Okay, we'll fix that today."

Clearly, Peter was siding with the homeless. What else was going to happen here?

I stood behind the counter and started handing out food.

If it had been me, I would never have accepted food from someone who had insulted me like that. But clearly, they had no choice. They took their meals in silence, sat at the tables, and quickly ate.

I started to feel uneasy. I had never been in a situation like this before. The only times I had felt hunger were during crash diets. Access to food had always felt like a given.

Maybe I should appreciate living with my parents more? Thanks to that, I'd been able to save some money. They surely meant well. And they had x-ray-like sensitivity when it came to my boyfriends. That picture with Ahmed had really made them grimace.

I decided to focus on the task at hand and not think about all of that.

Robert

I was sitting on a chair next to Greg's bed, pouring my whole heart and all my declamation skills into the words I was reading aloud.

"...The knife occupied a place in the picture, he decided, and would show well, with a sort of gleam, in the light of the stars..."

"I need scissors, not a knife," the old man interrupted. "Need to prepare soup for my funeral. Help! Nurse, help! He's so boring, I might die here today!"

The nurse appeared after a few such outbursts.

"Shut up, Greg! Or no dessert today!" she threatened.

That clearly enraged him.

"You're abusing my rights! You'll see—my revenge is coming."

"Maybe all this shouting isn't really necessary?" I tried to calm the situation.

"Try spending some time here, and you'll see—you'll be shouting too. Soon," Greg replied.

I started again from the last sentence I had read.

"...The knife..."

"Read me the last page," Greg interrupted bluntly. "You really could have chosen something more interesting. My patience wore thin after I hit ninety."

I looked at the last page.

"...This hurt was not death, was the thought that oscillated through his reeling consciousness. Death did not hurt. It was life, the pangs of life, this awful, suffocating feeling; it was the last blow life could deal him..."

I thought about my own life—something that could probably have been summarized in just a few sentences.

But Greg quickly snapped me back to reality.

"Honestly, I don't want you to read the whole book. I got the scissors!"

He pulled two pairs of nail scissors out of a drawer and handed one of them to me, along with half of the remaining blanket.

"You can help from one side. It'll go faster."

"I'm not in a hurry," I replied.

Greg started to laugh.

"I used to say the same... Thought I had all the time in the world. So I wasn't in a hurry with anything. I was going to start everything in retirement. But then..."

He began silently cutting diamond shapes from the quilt.

Obediently, I started cutting diamonds on my side of the blanket too.

"You're doing it crooked," Greg commented on my effort.

"Then?" I prompted, trying to distract him from my poor crafting skills.

"I didn't have enough money to travel. I lost the passion to do anything, to be honest. Life sucks. Maybe if I had another chance, I'd live it better... Maybe I'd celebrate each day. Each one is precious... If I could tell you the secret of life, it would be very simple. You just..."

The old man's head slumped back slightly. His hands went still.

"A nap? I'm fine with that, as long as you don't snore," I remarked—unaware that the old man had just passed away.

I continued cutting diamonds in silence, which turned out to be a very meditative activity.

Soon, I drifted off by myself, asleep with the scissors in one hand and a diamond of quilt in the other, still sitting in the chair.

Angela

"Make it nice! I have a job interview tomorrow," commented George.

I froze for a moment, scissors in one hand and tufts of long-untrimmed hair in the other.

"Really? Where?" I asked.

"At the university. I'm going to continue my research career."

"Yeah, sure," I said, continuing to cut the unruly locks.

"By the way, I have lice."

I instinctively jumped back.

"Or maybe not."

"So do you have them or not?" I asked, slightly annoyed.

I was supposed to be wallowing in my own depression right now, wrapped in a blanket and holding a mug of valerian tea—not scissors and a homeless man's hair.

"I have a PhD in Philosophy," George began to pontificate, a certain bitterness in his voice. "You won't believe me, because you're the type who likes to label everything and everyone. It's more likely for you to believe I have lice than a degree."

I started cutting again.

"Please don't talk. You're moving your head, and I can't cut your hair properly," I replied flatly.

"Are you grateful for what you have?"

"I don't answer personal questions," I responded.

A homeless woman approached us—probably George's partner.

"You're doing this wrong!" she yelled at me.

"I used to cut my brothers' hair," I said.

"Let me guess. They were much younger, and once they started school, they didn't want your haircuts anymore?" the woman mocked.

"Is it that bad?" George apparently cared about his appearance.

"Apparently, she doesn't care."

George took the shaver from me and finished the haircut himself.

Another homeless man took it next, ignoring me, and started shaving his own head.

"Your idea was great," I heard Peter's voice. "But it looks like you're going to lose your bet. They can handle the task themselves."

Robert

I woke up suddenly and realized that Greg was dead.

"Help! Help! Nurse!" I started shouting, trying to feel a pulse on the old man's wrist.

I heard a nurse's voice from the hallway.

"Shut up! That's not funny!"

"He died!" I yelled, running out into the corridor.

Robert

I stood with the nurse next to Greg's bed, surrounded by the scattered diamond shapes cut from the blanket.

"Oh my God! Why didn't I see it coming!" the woman cried.

"Yes. He was screaming every few minutes for your help!" I expressed my outrage.

"He's been screaming like that for the past few years! How was I supposed to know..."

"I'll report this to his family."

"He has no family," the woman sobbed. "They all died many years ago."

Something didn't sit right with me.

"Or maybe you convinced him to write his will in your favor? He definitely talked about his family!" I tried to unravel the mystery.

The nurse stopped crying. She looked at me.

"Which charity did you say you were from, again?" she asked suspiciously.

Angela

I sat at the table, jotting down whatever nonsense George was mumbling under his breath.

"Are you really going to print them for me?" he asked, worried.

"We haven't completed the hobbies section yet," I replied evasively.

"That's not so important. After printing the CVs, can you please deliver them to this address? The postman might bend them. It has to look perfect!" George fretted. Behind him, a few people in the queue were getting impatient.

"Yes, I can do it," I replied. "Who's next? Who needs a CV? Has anyone already finished their cover letter?"

Robert

What a mess. I was sitting in the nursing home, handcuffed to the bed of a dead man. Next to me, a police officer was taking notes and asking questions.

"Could you repeat—what was your relation to the deceased?"

"We're not related," I answered. The fewer words, the better.

"So, what were you doing here exactly?"

"Just a good deed."

"Do you support euthanasia?" the officer asked, testing me.

"Everyone, at least once in life, has wanted to kill everyone on this planet. You've never felt like that?"

I felt I was digging myself deeper.

"That's an interesting theory. Would you like to make a formal statement?"

The officer remained completely professional. Not a hint of confession about any murderous urges from his side.

"I just wanted to spend a few hours volunteering. To read and bring joy to someone. I bet they're all lonely here," I started explaining.

"But safe and alive. We just had a report from the hospital. The cause of death is still unknown."

"I know my rights. You haven't arrested me, yet you cuffed me to a bed. I'm going to—" I began to protest.

"Stay here. I'm going to discuss something with my superiors."

The officer left for the hallway.

I quickly opened Greg's drawer. It was full of thumbtacks, scissors. There was also a knife and a bar of chocolate.

I tried to open the handcuffs with a thumbtack, but I wasn't a criminal, and this definitely wasn't one of my top skills. Frustrated, I yanked my arm. The bed creaked loudly. The frame shifted slightly. I ducked down to check it out. The pipe I was cuffed to was loose. God must have loved lunatics, I thought.

I slid the handcuff off. Luckily, the officer had only cuffed one hand.

I was on the ground floor. I quietly approached the window. No bars. I wrestled with it for a moment, but soon I was in the garden.

My stomach growled. It might be a long night. Silently, I returned, grabbed the bar of chocolate—and vanished into the darkness of the green shrubs.

Robert & Angela

I was walking calmly down the street, trying to look like a respectable citizen while hiding the handcuff on my wrist inside my coat pocket, when suddenly I heard the steady rhythm of footsteps on the empty street. I turned around, and who did I see?

"Bum Watcher? Are you that much of a pervert?" I asked.

Angela flared up.

"Are you stalking me again?"

"Where do you live?"

The woman stopped next to me. I caught the scent of her perfume—of course, it was strong and oriental. Like she was trying very hard to come across as a powerful woman. But I had seen her crying too many times. And then she opened her mouth and ruined whatever good impression she was making.

"I think I'm going to report you to the police."

I glanced instinctively over my shoulder.

"I have every right to be here. I live on this street. And you?"

"If you think I'm going to tell you my address..."

"You don't live here, do you?"

"I'm still volunteering..." she started to explain.

It was all very naïve. And all the stress of the last few hours began boiling over. I burst into a slightly hysterical laugh.

Then I launched into a tirade:

"So, first of all—it's you who's stalking me. There's strong evidence that you've been following me, not the other way around. And second—you didn't even pass the volunteering test. There are no homeless people here, no charities on this street!"

Angela pulled out an envelope and waved it triumphantly in front of my face.

"What's that?" I asked.

"My volunteering task! I had to deliver it to number 9, flat 3. I had five more minutes. I could walk slowly—I'd complete the task on time! And you? No dementia care homes here, I guess."

"That's my address. I'll take it from here."

I took the envelope from Angela's hand and raised it high in the air.

"Ha! Four hours and fifty-five minutes of volunteering. Almost passed!"

Angela tried to grab the envelope, but she was too short.

"It's theft! If you don't give it back immediately..."

I pulled out my driver's license and showed it to her. It had the same address as the one on the envelope.

"I don't get it! It's fake! You were stalking me! It's a conspiracy! Show me a different ID."

"I've got my debit and credit cards, but you don't exactly look trustworthy," I replied.

"Neither do you," Angela said, spotting the handcuffs dangling from my wrist.

We stared at each other in silence.

"Are you a criminal or something?" she asked.

"If I were, do you think I'd admit it?" I replied.

Angela shrugged. Clearly, she'd had a tough day, and my little misadventures no longer impressed her.

"If you let me hold the envelope for the next few minutes, I won't say at the meeting that you failed the test," she said.

I handed her the envelope.

"Deal."

We walked in silence.

"You could say something!" Angela snapped.

"They say silence is golden, and speech is silver."

"What happened during your volunteering? Did they kick you out?"

"I had to leave. And if escaping before the police counts, then I've got two more minutes left to pass my test."

Suddenly, I spotted a slowly approaching police car. I stopped and kissed a surprised Angela. Naturally, she hit me—this time with her backpack.

The police car let out a quick burst of its siren and stopped next to us.

Inside were two policewomen. Great. Absolutely busted.

One of them lowered the window and asked Angela:

"Hey, love, are you okay?"

"She's just volunteering," I chimed in.

"I didn't ask you."

"One more minute..." I whispered.

"Yeah, I did it voluntarily," Angela said reluctantly—raising even more suspicion.

One of the officers got out of the car and walked over to Angela.

"Did he just threaten you?"

"No. We're a happy couple. I just remembered he was staring at that blonde woman on the bus."

But the policewoman clearly smelled deception from a mile away.

"You can tell me anything. We can stop this!" she continued her interrogation.

"Don't you think I'm the victim here?" I protested. "I was just attacked with a heavy backpack! Females can be predators too! And now there are three of you!"

"He had a bad day," Angela said with a smile.

The policewoman walked back to the patrol car.

They sat there, both officers staring at us intensely.

"Would you like some coffee?" I asked Angela.

"A few more seconds, I'll give you this envelope and—"

"—and the cops will be curious why you left me right next to my own house. We're a happy couple, remember?"

Angela

I sat at the table while Robert was grinding coffee. I glanced around the kitchen, searching for anything at all to comment on so I wouldn't have to sit there in awkward silence.

After a moment, I spotted a familiar shape.

"You have the same shitty toaster," I commented.

Robert turned around, surprised.

"Pardon?"

"It makes me cry sometimes... the toast always comes out burnt..."

Suddenly, I burst into tears. I tried to hold back the sobs, but the pressure only reminded me of every other time I'd held back tears. I completely broke down. There was no stopping it.

Robert looked at his toaster.

"This one undercooks them. I have to toast everything twice. We can swap, if it'll make you stop crying."

I almost choked on my own sorrow.

And as if my humiliation weren't enough already, the doorbell suddenly rang.

"Oh no, you have guests..."

I covered my face with my hands, desperately trying to calm myself down.

Robert looked genuinely surprised.

"I wasn't expecting anyone..."

Robert

I heard the sound of a key turning in the lock. The door opened.

It was Becky. She walked into the kitchen as if she still lived there.

She looked at the tearful Angela, and—mimicking her gesture—covered her own face with her hands.

"Oh! Another emotional scene in the kitchen?" she said. I was right. She *was* a psychopath. Maybe she had come to kill me. Good thing I had a witness.

"What are you doing here?" I asked.

"I forgot something."

Becky took a plastic bag out of her handbag and opened a kitchen cabinet.

"Do you prefer I take the oregano or the mixed herbs?" she asked.

"You're joking, right? Did you come here to talk?"

Becky pulled out a paper with a list of everything in the kitchen. Oregano was first on the list.

What a relief. She hadn't come to kill me—she just needed to spice up her life.

Angela stopped crying. Probably from the shock.

Becky reached for the coffee grinder.

"Yes, take it. I was about to throw it out anyway," I commented.

"It's new and it cost over a hundred quid," Becky scolded.

"Yeah, take it."

Becky paused, turned around, and reached for the recipe books.

"They stay!" I said, stepping between her and the books.

Becky started yelling.

"I can take whatever I want!"

I walked over to the window and looked outside. The police car was still there. Becky emptied the spices from the bag and took all the cookbooks.

I opened the window.

"Help! There's a robber in Flat 3! Help!" I started screaming. I wasn't giving her those books.

The policewoman flipped me the middle finger from the patrol car.

They started the engine and drove off.

"Unbelievable!" I commented.

Becky, intrigued, stepped up next to me and spotted the police car.

"Me? A robber? Do you know what that would mean for my career?"

Got you, I thought—and immediately began speaking directly to the weak spot I'd just uncovered.

"This is basically my flat. You have no legal right to be here anymore. Leave the books."

Becky froze. Then she started taking the books out. She reached for the oregano.

"Leave the oregano. It'll remind me of this dull, boring life with you. I had to buy tons of it just to make life feel spicier."

Becky looked at me and slowly threw the oregano into the sink.

"You want war? You'll get into a war! Your little servant won't save you."

"Servant? What is this, the 19th century? Or have you completely lost it?"

Becky pointed at Angela.

"If she's not your servant, is this your new girlfriend?"

"Yes. We're heading to Paris soon."

"I bet she'll need Parisian clothes," Becky said, laughing as she looked at Angela's outfit.

"But they rarely carry XXXL. Primark might do the job, considering she's temporary. Did she drug you? You never liked the heavyset!"

Angela stood up.

"If I killed her, would you help me bury the body?" she asked.

Becky started slowly walking toward the door.

"She's crazy!"

"That wouldn't be necessary..." I began.

"Ha! You still love me, you fool!" Becky shouted.

"It wouldn't be necessary to deal with hiding the body. She entered without permission, she's clearly not in her right mind, we're scared... I think that's enough for the police. And honestly, I don't care about court trials."

Angela, making a frightening face, took a few slow steps toward Becky. The smudged mascara only added to her credibility. Becky forced a nervous smile, but quickly backed away.

"You're nuts! I don't know what kind of drugs you two are on, but everyone will hear about this! I'll make your life not worth living!"

Becky fled, slamming the door behind her.

I lowered my head.

"It already is..." I commented on my life.

"Do you have whisky?" Angela asked. Another woman who wanted something.

I sat down in the other chair.

"Yeah... but you can buy it on your way home," I replied.

"Everyone would see that I've been crying. Do you have any human traits? By the way, if you cared about someone more than yourself, maybe you'd actually feel better."

"Is that what your psychotherapist told you in those bonus minutes—stolen from my life? I don't drink with the enemy. I don't have many rules left, but let's stick to that one."

"It's good to set boundaries. You should try doing that with your ex."

Angela picked up her backpack and left my place.

I took the whisky out of the cupboard, ice from the freezer, and made myself a drink with Coke. I put on the most depressing track I could find and began sipping my drink.

Angela

I was going to be late again, although this time it might actually have been good for me (and extended my life). I burst into the headquarters of the Suicides Club.

Coach and Robert were already sitting in their chairs. The sight of Robert finally stirred some emotion in me—unfortunately, negative. Strange that he hadn't choked on that pathetic whisky of his. He was probably hungover. But the bastard didn't show a trace of it—on top of that, he was annoyingly handsome. Evil people always seemed to have some redeeming qualities, just enough to cause harm and spread illusions among as many people as possible.

Without saying hello, I dropped into a chair.

Robert had taken my usual spot—of course he had.

Coach spoke up.

"So you both did not complete the first task."

How the hell did that weasel know we had failed the assignment? It had cost me a lot of nerves; it should have counted. Probably Robert had snitched on me.

"I did! I spent fucking five hours of my life listening to that nonsense!" I exploded angrily.

"And you?" Coach asked Robert. Was this some kind of setup, or what?

"I had to listen to even more sophisticated nonsense," Robert began rambling. Thankfully, Coach cut him off.

"You both failed. Neither of you spent the full five hours volunteering, and you didn't achieve any enlightenment."

Enlightenment. He probably had those regularly—maybe he was the guru of some cult? My parents would definitely have been alarmed by the things this guy said. Robert seemed to think the same.

"Oh! Don't tell me you're about to recommend joining some cult now."

"No. I'm not that religious. But I do believe life has some meaning. Unless, of course, someone hired me as a hitman, to take it. Then—sorry!"

The conversation was starting to veer off into some weird territory, so I asked something rational.

"If we failed, are we out of the program?"

Coach looked at me for a moment. Then he fixed his gaze on the old mirror hanging in the ballet hall.

After a pause—which looked as if he were deep in thought—he responded,

"No. We're going to continue. Our organization is short on money. For some unknown reason, people nowadays prefer to kill themselves rather than others. Not enough orders! So, we're going with the flow. Business adaptation is one of the levers of success."

"So... the money we're giving you—could it be used to kill someone else?" Robert asked.

Typical. A weak man who probably couldn't solve his problems through conversation, looking for easy solutions. He probably wanted to get rid of his ex.

"No. But I can give you that opportunity.

But you only have ten minutes, starting now, to decide."

The Coach pointed at the clock on the wall.

It was ten to six.

Robert

It was six o'clock. The Coach was yawning.

We were sitting there, quietly murmuring the names on our enemy lists.

"Okay. Time's up," the Coach interrupted us.

"It's a matter of life and death! We should get more time for this!" I protested.

"If you can't immediately point to one person, it means you're the one responsible for all your life's flaws..." he snapped back at me, the jerk.

"I've got five people!" Angela said.

"I can give you a discount," replied the Coach.

"Would it be... like... guaranteed?" the woman asked.

"Our organization has a 98% success rate on fulfilling orders," the Coach replied proudly.

Angela put her list back in her handbag.

"I think it'd be cheaper just to tell them they're assholes," she said—and quite sensibly, too.

But the Coach wasn't thrilled with her approach to life.

"Eh. You're not our ideal type of client. What about you?" he asked me.

I also stashed my list, crumpling the piece of paper into my pocket.

"I have to admit, she's right. Hiring someone to harm or kill these idiots would make me a coward. A confrontation might be more satisfying. And I've got little to lose," I said.

The Coach looked at us as if we were some alien species.

"What about the last task? Did either of you suddenly find a life purpose over the past few days?" he asked after a moment of silence.

"Life is miserable. When I was 30, I still believed it could lead to something. That I'd become happy. But do you know what happened?"

Her question lingered in the air, so I jumped in.

"Time sped up!"

"Exactly!" Angela confirmed. "The last ten years flew by in the blink of an eye. I'm not happy at all. But I am wiser—and I know what to expect now!"

The Coach started to laugh.

"So, can you predict my future in that case?" he asked Angela.

"You'll end up in prison, I guess."

"She's right," I began speaking almost involuntarily. "I have to agree. I didn't expect her to be that smart. But she knows what I know. Even the sunniest days will turn grey. And those so-called 'happy moments'—they're a trap. A trap of life, to make people provide for kids or grandkids. But I don't have any, so I can see through these nature tricks."

This time, the Coach seemed genuinely pissed, because he started yelling.

"I can't listen to either of you! A few more minutes and I'll have stomach ulcers. You're so bitter! So, your next task—you have to arrange a date for each other. Maybe a little 'love's spell' will fix your minds. Dismissed!"

"A date?"

Poor girl had probably never been on one—definitely not a proper one. But I wasn't going to help her. Actually, I planned to set her up. She deserved it.

"I don't know how I could convince anyone to go out with her. And she'll probably mix me up with some monster," I said, guessing the hostility went both ways, and hoping to talk the Coach out of the idea.

But he wouldn't budge.

"You've got one week. Now get out!" he yelled.

Angela

I was marching behind Robert toward the bus stop. Did he always have to walk at the same pace as me?

Apparently, it annoyed him too, because he turned around to look at me. At that exact moment, my gaze happened to be fixed on his butt—only because his phone was sticking out of his back pocket. Wasn't he afraid of theft?

But now he would probably think I was staring at his slim—though admittedly shapely—butt again.

I was the first to break the silence.

"Maybe we can help each other with our lists?" I asked.

Robert looked at me, distracted.

"Which lists?" he asked.

Which lists? This guy had been ready to wipe out half of London, and if it hadn't been for the ten-minute time limit, he probably would've taken out half the UK population.

"I saw you! You wrote down like ten names!" I said diplomatically.

"Your list was longer," he snapped back.

We walked a few meters in silence. I probably shouldn't have brought it up.

But suddenly, Robert broke the awkward silence.

"I don't want to kill those people. At the top of the list are my parents. But a confrontation would be nice—and yes, you can help me."

"You were ready to hire a hitman to kill your parents?"

I was shocked by what I had just heard.

"To be honest, I blame them for the end of my relationship. Becky was never good enough for them. But really, who is perfect?"

"The one who wanted to get your oregano was a bit weird," I said diplomatically.

"She used to be sweet and nice. I think our breakup made her a bit... extravagant..."

"So how exactly am I supposed to help you?" I asked.

"Oh! Old-school trick—pretend to be my girlfriend. When my parents see you, they'll start missing Becky for sure. Maybe all isn't lost."

Robert

And so there we were, sitting together in my parents' living room.

Angela and my mother were on the sofa. My father and I sat in the neighboring armchairs.

Surprisingly, my parents were *thrilled* with Angela. The plan had completely backfired.

"So, when are you getting married?" my mother suddenly asked.

"What?" I responded, a bit rudely—but considering I had been half-convinced I'd started hallucinating from Becky's leftover pills, I'd say I was holding myself together quite well.

"I wanted to ask the same thing. You two look perfect together," my father added.

Had they time-traveled back to their hippie days and taken something?

This was the first time they had liked any woman I'd ever brought home.

Maybe I should have asked what they were on.

"Becky wasn't perfect?" I probed.

"Becky acted like she had... issues. Lots of them," my mother began.

"I'm Muslim, we can't have a wedding. Robert's Christian, so..." Angela jumped in—thankfully.

A strange silence fell over the room.

"You didn't tell her yet?" my father asked, surprised.

"Tell me what?" Angela looked mildly intrigued.

"I'm actually Jewish. You see, things moved so fast I didn't have time to mention it."

We both burst out laughing hysterically.

"Now I get why we don't like each other," Angela finally said.

My mother hugged her. What the hell was going on?

"You two look so adorable together. We're not that old-fashioned. The wedding could be just—"

"They just met, let's give it a minute," my father cut her off, thankfully.

And that was when my mother started shouting—for the first time in my life, I saw her like this.

"I want grandchildren! And did you notice how relaxed Robert is when he's with Angela?"

I decided to evacuate. I was no longer interested in whether my parents had discovered some hippie miracle drug that made life look as if it were bathed in a rosy glow.

Angela

Robert's parents were waving goodbye from the doorstep. We waved back and picked up our pace.

After walking a few yards, I started to giggle.

"So... the top of the list... I think I get it now. They actually scared me—and I'm only pretending to be your girlfriend. What was Becky like?"

Robert seemed dazed by something and immediately protested.

"No. I don't get it. It's probably their new tactic. They've both been studying war theory—ancient to modern—to improve their chess game."

I stopped walking, involuntarily.

"They're good chess players?" I asked, intrigued.

Robert seemed to be reading my mind.

"We are not going back! You can play chess somewhere else—with me."

"It's hard to find someone who even knows the basic rules. And finding good players is rare..."

"We can play at the café on the next corner. Just—please—let's get away from here! I'll beat you in three moves."

Robert

I had probably overdone it with that three-move comment—but to be fair, it had been a while since I last played chess. Angela was right; it really *was* hard to find someone these days who was even a decent playing partner.

What was she planning with that knight and her queen?

"It's been five minutes," Angela said mockingly.

"Who's at the top of your list?" I asked, trying to change the subject—and suddenly I heard some absurd story.

Had she made it up? Probably not. Becky had been weird too, with her attempted oregano heist.

Robert

"Do you think I might make him jealous? He's getting married," I asked, as Angela finished her story.

"You probably won't—but we can try," Angela said, and just like that, any fresh affection I had for her instantly dropped to zero.

"I don't really have a choice. But first, let's sort out our dates. I'm sorry to say that the only single person in my circle is... my boss," she added.

"Do you have a picture?" I asked, trying not to show that my male ego had taken a hit from her offhand comment.

Angela pulled up a festive work photo and showed it to me.

I whistled out loud. The woman in the photo was stunning.

"She's a little bitch," Angela said, obviously jealous.

"Doesn't matter. Doesn't matter. Well, my boss is also single. I'll arrange a date for you—somewhere cheap..."

"And where are you going?" she asked quietly.

"There's this new, posh place with a rooftop garden that just opened..." I began describing the plants, the ivy, and the view of London.

Angela checkmated me on the board and started packing up to leave.

"Whenever I start to like you even a little, it turns out you're a complete jerk. You've got my phone number. Set up my date," she said softly, and walked out of the café.

For a moment, I didn't get what had just happened.

It took five minutes before the lightbulb went off in my head.

"Eh... you don't get it. He never pays on dates..." I muttered to myself, putting the chess pieces back into the box.

Robert

I was sitting on the rooftop of the Pretty Frog restaurant. At every table, there was an electric heater with a screen in the middle simulating flames. So many simulations and imitations everywhere.

But the view of a beautifully lit-up London made up for it. A few couples, with restaurant blankets draped over their shoulders, were chatting quietly.

Michaela actually looked beautiful. I decided to start a conversation.

"Oh my God! I don't believe it! There are a few stars above us!"

Michaela responded with a slightly sharp tone.

"Playing romantic so early? Doesn't quite match the description of you. Cold, arrogant but rich..."

"I'd rather not hear the rest of that description. It's just unusual to see stars here because of all the city lights!" I replied.

"Hmm. I didn't notice."

Suddenly, she started playing with a strand of her hair, staring at the entrance. I turned around—and who did I see? Angela and my boss.

"Oh no!" I blurted out.

Angela saw us too, and it was clear she wasn't pleased. She hesitated for a moment, then finally walked up to our table.

"Just wanted to say hello. I didn't expect you to be here at the same time."

"Please come join us," Michaela said in a commanding tone. "So far, we were talking about stars."

"What?" Angela was clearly surprised.

My boss stepped forward to greet us. He kissed Michaela's hand.

"So charming!" said the blonde beauty. Apparently, that was better than stars.

Angela blushed. It seemed her hand didn't receive the same treatment.

"I like romantic men," Michaela continued.

"Really?" slipped out of my mouth.

A waiter appeared.

"Would you like me to put two tables together?"

"That's not the best idea," I protested.

"Jealous?"

I probably wasn't going to like Michaela.

She nodded "yes" to the waiter. The waiter didn't ask anyone else and started assembling the two tables together.

Angela

Robert was eating tortilla chips from his chili with his fingers. He was watching the couple across from us like he was in a cinema, eating popcorn.

I preferred to stare at my salad.

Across from him, Michaela was eating chicken and placing the bones next to her plate, directly on the table. Robert's boss looked at her, astonished.

"Yes, discipline is the best way to achieve success. Shame we have to force it into the lives of our employees," said Michaela in a nasal tone.

"Yes, yes."

Staring at her, my date would probably have been just as thrilled if she had told him she laundered dirty money. Nothing seemed to reach him.

"Imagine how lost they would be without us," Michaela continued.

"Yes, right."

"Oh, you are so smart. I like eloquent men."

Robert started choking on a chip. I hit him forcefully on the back. It helped.

"I'm going to tell my parents you hit me. They're already too crazy about your presence in our family," he complained — probably because I had hit him too hard, but he deserved it.

Michaela started to choke. Robert's boss looked worried, then hit Michaela on the back in a similar manner.

Michaela's face ended up on her plate. She was still choking.

The waiter appeared and helped her using a traditional, elegant technique, known as Heimlich maneuver.

Michaela breathed heavily. Robert watched the spectacle with his mouth open. I preferred to look at the stars.

Michaela finally got her breathing under control. Suddenly, she roared like a lion:

"You're getting married? What the hell was that? This pairing with the bosses? A social experiment?"

"I'm impressed by its results."

Robert's comment didn't help, so I quickly denied it.

"We're not getti—"

"You small, manipulative bitch," my boss interrupted me. "We'll discuss this at work."

Michaela stood up. Food was still on her face, her dress, and the blanket. She stormed off.

Robert's boss, without a word, tried to sneak after her.

"Pay for yourself and your queen!" Robert shouted after him.

"She's your queen. I only pay for myself on first dates. But your experiment... this was too much!" Robert's boss said indignantly. He left without paying the bill.

Robert

"You missed a lot while staring at that green lettuce. You should've seen her face when he hit her!" I said to Angela. I hadn't laughed that hard in ages — my stomach muscles actually hurt.

Other couples looked concerned and started chatting even more quietly than at the beginning of the evening.

The waiter appeared with the bill.

"That was worth it. Best comedy show ever," I said, looking at the check.

"I might get fired," Angela wasn't amused.

And then it hit me — we were planning to kill ourselves. In the face of meeting either nothingness or God, what did such trivial things as an outraged boss even matter?

I started laughing even louder.

"So what? You'll be dead in a few weeks!"

Other people stopped talking and stared at us in shock. I pulled out my credit card.

Suddenly, the restaurant owner appeared.

"It's on the house, but I would kindly ask you to leave. Also, please don't come back."

"Pardon?" I said, surprised.

"You've just been banned."

Angela

I was trying to find the number of some cheap taxi companies. I hadn't needed one for years. I had stopped going to parties to focus on my career and my life. It probably hadn't done me much good, but at least I didn't have problems with alcohol.

Speaking of alcohol!

Robert had just come out of the shop, lugging a bag with a few bottles of wine.

"Let's go!" he said to me.

"Since when have we been friends? I'm going to order a taxi home," I replied, showing him my phone screen with the search results.

"This time I'm not going to drink alone. And it'll be hard to find someone free. It's Friday night," he answered.

So the only reason was his lack of access to other people. Let him shove it.

"I don't care about your drinking problem," I said out loud.

"You're funny. Come with me, or I'll get your address from Michaela and send my parents to you."

"I doubt she'd speak to you."

Robert took out his phone.

"Look and learn," he said to me. He called Michaela, who, to my surprise, picked up.

"Hi, are you all right? My brother's a plastic surgeon... Yes, this Jake."

Robert listened to Michaela for a while.

"Yes, I can arrange an appointment, but I need Angela's address. She left something..."

"I didn't!" I cut into the conversation. He was doing too well with this.

"Shush! This is a private conversation. These call girls nowadays... sometimes they're too mouthy. You were one of them? Really? Okay, I'll keep it a secret."

He winked at me while I tried to process this revelation.

"Keeley Street? And the house number? Thank you."

He ended the call.

"Now you know something important about your boss. Feeling a bit better?" he asked.

"You made it up," I protested.

"Maybe. But I know your address. Do you prefer a visit from my parents, or a conversation over chess and wine?"

Robert

We were sitting in my kitchen. A chessboard was laid out on the table. Angela hardly even looked at the board, yet she made her moves in a split second. Unlike me. The silence was starting to bother me, so I struck up a conversation—hoping at the same time that Angela might make a mistake.

"I like to lose. You know, you always learn something." I made another move with a pawn, because nothing else came to mind. "Have you ever been banned?" I asked Angela.

"From the co-op shop," she replied.

I stared at her, slightly shocked. She noticed and started explaining.

"It was a long trip by train, a long queue. I thought my bladder would explode. And I still had half a mile walk back home. I threw the money on the counter and ran out of the shop."

"Did you make it?" I asked.

"Yes, at the last second."

"I meant the escape from the shop!"

"Yes. But the next shopping trip was very embarrassing. I was accused of not paying the full amount. I wanted to pay the imagined 'extra money,' but they were too furious. I've been banned ever since."

I looked at the chessboard. It didn't look good. A few more moves and I'd probably lose. Suddenly, a Machiavellian plan came to my mind.

"Would you like to visit that shop?" I asked.

Angela

Robert was doing a bit of shopping, picking out some snacks. From behind the counter, the shop assistant was watching us. Robert headed for the counter.

Somewhat reluctantly, I followed him. The wine was bubbling in my veins, making my head a little dizzy. On the other hand, the adrenaline was working too. I was curious what the shop assistant would say.

To my surprise, he greeted me very kindly.

"Hello, love. Haven't seen you for a while..."

Robert suddenly threw money onto the counter, grabbed the shopping, and shouted to me:

"Run! Run!"

We dashed outside and jumped into a taxi parked nearby—his friend's.

"Go, go, go!" Robert yells at the driver.

The taxi sped away. The furious shop assistant ran out of the shop, but the car was already too far.

"What the hell was that? A robbery?" asked the driver, sounding slightly stressed.

"I paid," Robert answered.

The driver looked uneasy. Seeing his face, I suddenly burst out laughing. Robert too.

"Maniacs," the driver commented.

We were laughing, unable to stop.

"Where should I drive?" asked the driver, who now looked rather disgusted with our stunt.

"What's your favourite place in London?" Robert asked me.

A wave of warmth flooded over me. I didn't know if it was the wine, the run, the adrenaline—or simply that someone was being nice to me.

"Opposite Big Ben," I answered, a little hesitantly. Maybe it was some sarcastic trick and Robert would shoot back with a nasty comment.

"It's broken at the moment," the driver remarked.

Meanwhile Robert looked surprised at my answer.

"Really? It's so popular..."

"I like to look at old buildings, and this one is one of the oldest here?" I began to explain.

"Not sure. Marek is a tourist guide, he should know."

"Kind of," the driver began, hesitantly. Then suddenly he changed the subject.

"How's that crazy bitch, the one who steals your psychotherapy time? Did you sort it?"

Sudden silence filled the car.

"Kind of," I answered for Robert.

The driver, Marek, stopped at the lights.

It was my chance. I quickly got out of the taxi and slammed the door behind me. I wove between cars until I reached the pavement.

And this could have been such a nice evening after all.

Robert

"Wow, this one is even crazier. Sorry about your bad luck, but women, you know, they..." Marek commented on Angela's exit.

"It's her," I replied quietly. And this could have been such a nice evening, I thought.

"This was the bitch? You're joking? I thought you two were a couple. I just didn't know how to ask—why you'd hidden it from me. Sorry, man. Sorry..."

"It's not your fault. I should have told you..."

"Maybe you should go after her, explain?" Marek pulled into a bus bay. The driver of the bus behind us started honking.

Apathy and plain exhaustion overwhelmed me.

"It doesn't matter," I answered.

Marek left the bus bay.

"By the way, I didn't know crime could unite people so much..." I muttered under my breath.

"You said you paid?"

"Kind of."

Robert

I sat in the Suicides Club room. There was no one there but me. A strange unease crept over me. For the first time in a long while, I was biting my lips.

The room was, surprisingly, very clean. Other details caught my eye too—the curtains were fresh, and they smelled faintly of fabric softener.

Angela and Coach weren't there. I glanced at my phone to check if I'd gotten the time wrong.

A message icon. It was from Coach.

I opened it, intrigued.

"I went on holiday. Your task is to arrange your own. No excuses, or someone close to you will die (for free). We're always thirsty for blood after holidays."

My unease exploded into rage. But there was no one and nothing to unload it on. In the heat of the moment, I typed a reply:

"You fucker! Don't involve my family in this! I'm done with your childish games. I quit!"

On my way out I gave a chair a hard kick—maybe they had hidden cameras here, and they'd see there was no joking with me.

The chair didn't even budge. It was probably bolted to the floor.

Defeated, I left. It must have looked downright pathetic.

Robert

I was walking through Trafalgar Square, drinking a double espresso. It was snowing—something that didn't happen here as often as the movies made it seem.

I was just passing a group of kids singing carols when I heard my mobile phone. It was Coach, ringing me on WhatsApp.

I stopped and picked up.

Coach was sitting with a drink on black sand. He must have gone somewhere to the Canary Islands.

"No leaving. This is one of the rules," he said quickly, as if suspecting I might hang up any second.

"Never heard of it," I replied.

"You didn't let me finish. You two are like a long-married couple, fighting about the color of the walls' paint."

I didn't answer. I saw his face change. Something had intrigued him.

"That's really interesting," he said, taking a big sip of liquid that looked like a mojito.

"I didn't say anything," I answered.

"Did you change your mind?"

"No. I still don't like her."

The old man burst into laughter.

"I was asking about your life-ending decision."

"I didn't think about it."

The kids next to me started singing louder.

I had had enough of all this Christmas cheer. Enough of Christmas altogether.

"Could you finally shut up, you little bastards?" I shouted at the children.

"You're an asshole!" one of them yelled back.

The kids started shouting in unison: *"Asshole! Asshole! Asshole!"*

Coach started laughing.

"I see that you've started to enjoy life."

He hung up.

The kids started pelting me with snowballs. It turned into a serious battle. I tried to fight back, but I was outnumbered.

What I hadn't noticed were the people who had been filming this battle.

Robert

I was lying alone in my enormous bed, watching the news on TV, previously encouraged to do so by my parents.

The news programme was broadcasting my escape, including the kids chasing me and bombarding me with snowballs.

I took a sip of Pinot Grigio.

"Little fuckers!" I commented.

The news presenter was tearing into me as much as possible within today's politically correct limits.

"As we can see, the Christmas spirit is *not* present in everyone. If anyone knows our Scrooge, give him a few hugs."

Of course, my phone started ringing immediately.

I wisely rejected the call from my parents, but I did answer the one from my boss.

"Do you want to hug me?" I asked.

"What? Are you drunk?"

Clearly, my boss wasn't up to date with the situation.

"Sorry, I thought you were watching the news."

"I was watching your performance data. They are not the best!"

"It's burnout. I need a few days off."

"No freaking way!"

My boss rarely used that kind of language — but honestly, what did I have to lose?

"I'm entitled to annual leave. I haven't had a holiday in three years! Now fuck off! I'm coming back on Monday," I snapped.

"This is Christmas time. All leave was booked eleven months in advance!"

"I'm ill. Bye."

I hung up.

It was quite an enjoyable call, actually!

I looked at my phone, suddenly a bit concerned.

I drank the rest of the wine in a few sips and chose Angela's number. She didn't answer.

Angela

I was looking at my old pictures. In most of them, I was dancing.

I stood up and looked at myself in the mirror.

The phone rang. It was Robert again.

I rejected the call.

A moment later, a text message came in — obviously from Robert. Who else would think about me, except this lunatic?

I read the message.

"This week we have to go on holiday."

I decided to call this jerk back. Let him feel my emotions and my disgust.

"I am not going anywhere with you!" I screamed into the receiver with fury.

"I didn't ask you out!" he replied, arrogant as always.

"You didn't. You asked me to go on holiday! That's an even more advanced proposal, don't you think?"

"I didn't — but it might be funny. Don't hang up, there is another rule. Probably one of many."

I hung up.

A new message arrived quickly:

"We can't quit. If we do, someone close to us will suffer."

I didn't reply.

I played the video again — the one where Robert threw a snowball at the kids.

At that moment, my mother entered the room, as always without knocking.

She noticed the video, frozen on Robert's close-up.

"The world is full of psychopaths. I hope God protects you from such men and sends you a good husband," she sighed.

I had enough of these religious wishes. God kept sending me problematic individuals — probably as punishment for childhood sins I no longer remembered.

I decided to disturb my mother's peace.

"I'm going on holiday with him," I announced.

And what did this woman do? She lifted her hands toward the ceiling in a thankful gesture.

"What? You're happy that I'm going somewhere with a psychopath?" I asked.

"I'm happy for you."

"He's Jewish," I added, providing the necessary detail that any decent Muslim mother would treat as a red flag — and immediately start discouraging the relationship.

And what did she say?

"Everyone must have some flaws," she replied, and left the room, apparently delighted.

A moment later I heard her shouting in the kitchen — in Farsi, thankfully, so the neighbours wouldn't understand:

"You won't believe it! She's getting married!"

And that's the moment I thought that I really needed a break from these nuts.

My phone rang again.

It was Michaela.

"This is so bad for the company PR!" she started screaming.

"What are you talking about?"

"Your fiancé! Please sort this out!"

"He's not my fiancé."

"So he's your husband? How did you get married? Who organised your wedding, you little traitor?"

"You can't fire me. You need me."

"Who said anything about ending your contract? By the way, it expires this year, and every employee can be replaced, my dear. There are hundreds of young, energetic girls prettier than you."

"I will need a few days off to sort it out," I replied calmly, as usual.

Robert & Angela

I decided to make use of Marek's services. And here I am now, dressed in white highlander clothes — I refused to put on the sheepskin coat — trying not to break my spine while performing some bizarre old-Polish dance contortions, including squat-kicking highlander steps.

It was announced to me that highlanders were supposedly a different breed of Poles anyway, something like mutated Scots.

Did I mention we ended up in some snow-buried village, one we only reached because we were driving right behind a snowplough?

While we were dancing, Marek was drinking yet another mulled beer with the dancing instructor.

I looked at Angela.

She was wearing a traditional highlander female dress. She looked pretty.

Both Marek and the dancing instructor were staring at her.

I must admit — she was doing well. Probably because she was a perfectionist.

She had just performed an advanced dance figure.

Meanwhile, I fell onto the ground.

Thankfully, Angela was too focused on her own performance to notice.

"This is horrible. This is a nightmare!" she declared.

"Try the male moves, they're really funny," I suggested, attempting a few *holubce*.

"Okay, folks, that's all for the folk dance lesson. Now let's practise it in a real scenario," Marek decided.

Angela & Robert

We were sitting in the dim room of a pub styled like an old highlander tavern.

Sipping mulled beer with raspberry syrup, I listened to Marek's voice as he sat beside me, gently holding me in his arms.

It was actually... pleasant.

Especially since Robert, sitting opposite us, looked utterly sour.

"I really like curvy women," Marek was proclaiming. "Here every girl is so skinny — Poland is like the kingdom of anorexia."

"Each of them looks like a top model! I feel like I'm in heaven. I think I'll move here..." Robert snapped back.

"After losing your job, it might be wise to live in a country with lower living costs," I agreed with his idea.

"I still *have* my job!"

"You committed fraud at the Co-op and terrorised a group of kids at Trafalgar Square," I shot back.

"He's a good man. I've known him for a long time. Very dedicated to his work," Marek began defending Robert.

Seeing I wasn't buying a word of it, he quickly changed the subject.

"You look so sexy," he said — and then leaned in to kiss me.

Robert glanced at us, stood up from the table, and walked to the bar.

He didn't see that I pulled away and the kiss never happened.

But maybe it was better that way.

Robert

Marek was definitely exaggerating. What does he even see in this Angela? Has the guy gone mad?

Well... she *does* have an interesting personality, and her eyes have that honey-like colour with tiny specks of darker brown...

Is this barmaid ever going to come to me?

She's definitely too skinny, even for my taste.

And she insists on ignoring me!

Suddenly, a delicate whiff of perfume reached me — maybe a bit cheap, but at least someone made an effort.

A blonde woman stood next to me: slim, long-haired, dressed in sports clothes.

I decided to strike up a conversation.

"Is the barman always so slow?"

"No English. Pardon? Not speak," the blonde replied.

Shame.

I instantly lost interest.

What good is beauty if I can't talk to her, can't even play chess with her?

Suddenly, music started — the kind that didn't require breaking your spine or legs.

The kind that allowed me to show that I could, in fact, dance.

"Do you dance?" I asked the blonde.

She nodded.

We went to a small dancing area where two couples were already struggling to keep up with the rhythm.

I started dancing with the blonde woman.

Suddenly, the music changed into a slow song.

The blonde began making slow, feline moves, and I must admit — I got into that slow dance quite easily.

I heard a commotion at one of the tables, but the blonde was kissing my neck at that moment, and my hands were on her buttocks.

I looked over her head and saw Marek dragging Angela toward the exit.

"Run! Run for your life!" he shouted to me, pointing behind me with his free hand.

I turned reluctantly.

Behind me stood a *copy* of the blonde — except this one was clearly a bearded man — reaching for a **ciupaga** that was a kind of local axe and a part of the interior décor.

Or maybe those axes were left there *on purpose*?

It was probably her twin brother — but that thought came later.

For now, I just saw a bearded guy who looked exactly like the person who had just been kissing me.

And he was majestically approaching us with an axe.

I pushed the blonde away — strangely, she stopped being attractive the moment I saw her bearded version — and I ran toward the door, hearing slightly faster footsteps behind me.

Angela and Marek were already in his car.

I slipped on the frosted pavement, trying to cover those few metres as fast as possible.

"You not finish dance! *Insult!*" I heard a male bass voice behind me.

I jumped inside.

Marek drove away.

I turned around to give the monster the middle finger — but instead, my jaw dropped at the sight of an axe flying toward the car.

It hit the back of the car, got stuck in it, but didn't cause any other damage.

"You shouldn't dance with her! But if you start, you must not leave her on the dance floor!"

"She behaved like a single woman!" I began explaining myself.

"That was her brother. You should ask him first."

"Oh my God, I thought *my* country was crazy. What's going on here?" Angela spoke up.

"Guys here look for any opportunity to fight," Marek began explaining the complexities of highlander culture. "Robert is a stranger. That's the main reason."

"What's the other reason?" I asked.

"We'll probably find out tomorrow.

That man was supposed to organise a sleigh ride for us," Marek replied.

Angela

There was snow on the road and hoarfrost on the fir trees. But we couldn't care less about the beautiful scenery. We were focused only on the tractor speeding down the forest road, with Robert's evil twin at the wheel.

We were at the back of the tractor—right at the very back—on three sleighs tied together with rope, all of them bouncing wildly behind the tractor. We were all screaming at the top of our lungs.

Suddenly, my sleigh hit a stone hidden under the snow, and I fell onto the road. Marek made a smart manoeuvre with the rope and his sleigh to avoid hitting me. Robert's sleigh, however, was heading straight for my body.

I closed my eyes.

A heavy thud landed right next to me. It was Robert—he had jumped out so he wouldn't run me over.

We heard a burst of manic laughter from the tractor, which didn't stop and soon disappeared into the forest. Robert got up, brushing snow off himself, and walked toward me as I sat stunned in the snow.

"Marek said it is a local entertainment for kids."

"Yes! I am okay! Thank you!"

"I'm sure you are, otherwise I would ask."

He offered his hand and helped me up.

We looked around.

"Do you remember to which country we were going?"

"Poland and Slovakia, that's what he said in London."

"I'm sure he'll come back to find us soon. But let's gather what we know. We are somewhere in the forest, in the mountains, somewhere in Eastern Europe, where people throw axes at you..."

"It's getting dark."

The sky had turned pinkish-yellow from the sunset. We looked around, worried. A distant wolf howl cut through the silence.

"Shit. Let's follow the tracks of the tractor. I'm sure if we follow it, we'll end up in some warm tavern," Robert said.

We started walking in the direction the tractor had gone.

Robert

So we were walking along the forest road. I was using my phone torch.

"Well, I would say it is quite romantic to get lost in the forest of a foreign country. There are stars in the sky."

Another wolf howl—this time a bit closer—interrupted my speech.

"Shit. Okay, it's a little bit scary," I added.

"There are not many news about Polish eaten by wolves," Angela said.

"Because the news reporters are treated with axes. Maybe it is a local way of welcoming guests."

"The wolves do not attack people. Not anymore," Angela said, probably trying to become an optimist.

"Okay, we may slow down in such case," I commented.

Angela looked around nervously.

"It's getting cold. Let's speed up," she said.

She seemed so vulnerable, that I took her hand into mine.

She looked at me, surprised.

"This way will be faster."

I threw out the quick explanation, because I had no idea why I had done it, nor how I was supposed to justify it now.

We walked, hand in hand.

Angela & Robert

We entered the pub. Marek was drinking vodka with the evil twin brother, both of them too drunk to notice us.

We sat at an empty table.

Suddenly, I started shivering.

"I thought you came from a land next to the Himalayan mountains and these temperatures feel like summer to you?" Robert commented.

"Your geography teacher should be fired."

"He was good. I wanted to be a globetrotter, discover new species of animals and plants in the jungles..."

"Stop pretending to be romantic," I interrupted.

"Okay, I'll go and try to discover a new mulled wine recipe. Be right back."

He returned with two big glasses of mulled wine and handed one to me.

"Thank you. You know, I never had a dream job as a kid. My mum always wanted me to get married as soon as possible..."

I didn't know why, but I started confiding in him.

"...so you became a wedding planner?" he replied in his usual sarcastic tone.

"And what happened to the globetrotting dream?" I asked.

"I collected herbs from the meadows. I wanted to become a botanist. Then my parents had a serious conversation with me. They said something like: 'We wish you well, so you can become either a doctor or a lawyer.'"

"So you could choose your profession."

"I'm a fraud investigator now, with a law diploma."

"Life sucks," I sighed.

"Life sucks!" Robert confirmed.

We clinked glasses.

Marek heard us, stood up with his drink, and raised a toast.

"Life starts after forty!" he shouted and downed his vodka.

His legs turned to jelly and he ended up under the table, unconscious.

"He's delusional," I stated.

"Same day all over again. Nothing new is going to start," Robert added.

I looked into his eyes and noticed tiny sparks in them.

I must have been tipsy, because I commented:

"I just realised you have nice eyes."

Robert

I choked a little on the wine.

"I am all nice," I replied quickly. "But you shouldn't give compliments to men. Maybe that's why you're single."

Before a blush had the chance to appear on my cheeks, I grabbed the empty glasses and headed toward the bar — but soon returned and sat back down.

Angela turned her head and spotted the blonde twin — the reason for my strategic retreat.

I handed her my debit card.

"It's contactless," I said.

Angela took the card with hesitation.

"Don't plan much around it. There are only a few pounds on this one."

"It's just... uncommon," she commented, and went to order more wine.

Angela

I stood there, trying to blend into the background, when the blonde female twin gave me *that* look — the one she reserved for women my size and expired yoghurt.

She leaned toward the barwoman, switched to English like a tourist with superiority issues, and announced:

"She's fat."

A few people turned their heads. Great. A small audience. Every woman's dream.

I ignored her — I'd had months of practice.

"Two big glasses of mulled wine," I said, as if everything were perfectly normal.

The barwoman squinted. "What?"

The blonde repeated, louder, enunciating like a malfunctioning translator:

"Big glass, because she is big."

And that was it. I turned toward her. My fist moved before my brain even filed the paperwork.

I hit her chin. She grabbed a fistful of my hair and yanked me backwards. Fire shot across my scalp.

We slammed into each other — claws, elbows, pure primitive instinct.

Somewhere behind me, I heard Robert shouting like an overexcited coach:

"Kick that skinny ass! Jab, jab!"

We crashed onto the sticky floor. I ended up on top, straddling her, adrenaline buzzing through my veins.

My punches weren't elegant, but they were mine — sloppy, furious, months of swallowed insults finally getting their moment.

The barwoman watched us with her arms crossed, unimpressed.

But when she noticed the blonde losing, she suddenly discovered her sense of justice.

"Stop! I'm calling the police!"

That was Robert's cue.

He grabbed our jackets in one swoop and hauled me up by the arm.

"Come on, Angela," he hissed.

We ran out into the cold night, laughter and leftover rage fizzing in my blood like electricity.

"How do you feel?" Robert asked.

"Great! It was like a therapy session the NHS would never approve," I burst into laughter.

My scalp burned. My knuckles tingled. And for the first time that evening, I felt warm.

Robert

We walked side by side, not talking. Angela had that silent, dangerous calm — the kind that comes right after someone punches a woman in a bar and doesn't blink about it. I didn't know whether to congratulate her or keep a safe distance.

Then it hit me — the absurdity of it all — and I started laughing.

Not because it was funny, but because the whole night felt like someone else's fever dream.

"Seventy-five," Angela said suddenly.

I frowned. "What?"

She didn't even look at me. "That's how many IQ points you just lost laughing like that."

God, I loved her deadpan brutality.

"I'd say something," I muttered, "but I'm afraid."

"Go on," she said.

"I am afraid," I repeated, but she waited anyway.

She always made you feel like confession was mandatory.

"I don't hit men," she added after a moment. "Well... they have to deserve it."

Fair enough. Most men probably did.

"You know," I said, choosing my words carefully, "you have this... wrestling gift. No offence, but all the girls here are skinny. We could organise a few fights and get rich."

She stared ahead, like money, violence, and opportunity were equally boring to her.

"What's the point?" she asked.

"Fun?" I tried. "How did you feel on top of her?"

She shrugged.

"I didn't want to be that cruel. It just popped out of me. Like a new person."

That part scared me a little — the way she said it so calmly, like there was an extra Angela living inside, waiting for the right insult to come out and kill someone.

So I said the first honest thing that came to mind:

"You want to end your life. Why not try this?"

She stopped walking.

The night around us went still.

For a moment, I wondered if I'd just become one of those men who deserved to be hit, the man pitching a business model to someone in existential crisis.

Angela

Marek stood in the middle of the hotel room like someone caught stealing his own wallet.

"Are you having a piss? And, regarding my behaviour, I was kidnapped yesterday, couldn't help you," he said.

Robert crossed his arms. "We saw you drinking with your offender."

Marek threw his hands up. "Believe me or not, I was forced to do this."

I watched them argue.

Suddenly Robert looked at him and muttered, "Is it possible?"

Robert

The barn smelled like sweat, mud and money people didn't really have.

Mountaineers were shouting over one another, throwing cash onto Marek's table like he was running a stock exchange in hell. The poor bastard looked ready to faint. I didn't blame him — if these guys lost their bets, Marek was going to be the first thing they reclaimed.

In the centre, two local fighters were crawling across the ground, bleeding and gasping like wounded wildlife. Neither of them had any business standing, much less fighting. One collapsed on top of the other, and the judge started counting to ten with the enthusiasm of a man who hated his job.

Then it was Angela's turn.

She was straddling a skinny Polish wrestler and beating her like she was kneading dough. The judge blew his whistle.

"That's not fair," he said. "Different weight. You will fight with two female warriors."

I jumped in before Angela could agree to anything stupid.

"Two for one? That's what's not fair!"

The judge didn't care. He blew the whistle again. "Out of the ring!"

Angela wasn't listening. Her eyes were blazing.

"Another one? I will smash them all!"

I looked at her and, for the first time that night, wondered if maybe this underground fight idea had been a mistake.

She grabbed the first girl like a rag doll and threw her to the ground. The second wrestler stepped into the ring, ready — and then suddenly froze.

"**Gliny!!! Spierdalamy!**" she screamed.

She bolted for the exit.

Everyone else went still for a heartbeat, like someone hit pause on reality.

"Looks like we won," I said, mostly to myself.

Then chaos. The entire crowd ran for their lives, the judge included, cash still in his pockets. The barn emptied in seconds, leaving the three of us standing in the debris of our almost-successful criminal enterprise.

"Hey!" I shouted after them. "Give us our money! Where do you think you're going?!"

No answer. Just silence.

I turned to Angela.

"It's not your fault," I said. "You did well."

That's when the barn doors exploded inward, ripped off the hinges like cardboard. Five policemen stormed inside.

"**Ręce do góry!**" It probably meant 'Hands up'. Seeing guns pointed at us, we raised our hands.

And just like that, our winning streak ended exactly the way I was afraid of — loudly, stupidly, and with police involvement.

Coach

The living room was warm and quiet.

I sat on the sofa, remote in hand, feeling the familiar itch of amusement rising in my chest as the reporter spoke in her polished, tragic voice:

"Two English citizens were deported today from Poland. Accused of illegal gambling, money laundering, and some other issues, they've been released due to lack of witnesses and proof, after three days spent in—"

I didn't catch the rest. Seeing pictures of Angela and Robert, I was laughing too hard.

The kind of laugh that squeezes your ribs and steals your breath, the kind of laugh you shouldn't be having about people you promised to kill.

My wife looked at me the way people look at malfunctioning machinery — curious, worried, mildly irritated.

"We spent some time together," she said, shaking her head, "but I still don't get your sense of humour."

I wiped my eyes, tried to breathe, and failed. How could I explain it to her?

Watching Angela and Robert turn an entire country into speculations and gossiping.

It was like watching two of my worst students finally apply what I taught them — just in the completely wrong context.

Coach

I couldn't stop laughing.

Angela and Robert sat opposite me, looking like the oxygen had been sucked out of them. Their usual sharpness replaced by something grey, flat — disappointment? exhaustion? Existential hangover? Hard to say. They both wore the same expression people have after realizing life is not only meaningless but also badly organized.

"The fraud investigator involved in money laundering!" I wheezed. "Ha! Ha!"

Robert rubbed his forehead like a man who had just discovered new categories of failure.

"I lost my job. The investigation is still ongoing. Some jerks, who kidnapped me earlier, paid a few pounds into my account. My money got frozen."

I tilted my head. "How are you going to pay us?"

"I don't care," he said, voice hollow. "It was fun. But I still don't see any reason to get up every day. To deal with all these tiny, shitty problems."

Angela nodded. "Yeah, it was fun. But we won't repeat it. That's the sad part."

I sighed theatrically.

"Just sign to an MMA club. It would solve half your issues. Though... It's problematic for me now. Originally, I wanted you to ask for a promotion at work, then get fired and insult your bosses. Very therapeutic. But you lost your jobs already. Completely out of sequence."

I smiled. "Now I owe you some explanation."

Robert leaned back. "Just get to the point."

I enjoyed how impatient he was. People always get impatient right before they hear the truth.

"You see," I said, hands spread like I was presenting a prize, "life can offer you much more than you expect... if you're brave enough to take it."

Angela frowned. Her voice was flat but polite in that way depressed people manage to be.

"We need an explanation. We're depressed, with no will to live, and you want us to be brave. Doesn't bravery require energy?"

"Of course it does," I said. "And that's why you've failed so far. You had boring lives. Safe lives. No high stakes. No adrenaline. You imagined something else — but kept choosing the dull option every time."

They stared at me, those two disasters I'd somehow grown fond of.

"I see potential," I continued. "So your last task is simple: write down your greatest fear — which is also your secret urge — and then do it."

Robert scoffed. "It's all just talking."

I smiled. He still didn't understand.

"You need to try," I said softly. "Otherwise... you will need to live. Or someone close to you will die."

The room fell silent. They finally listened.

Robert

We were standing outside the Club, still buzzing with the aftertaste of the Coach's madness, and Angela was doing that thing where she tried to sound reasonable while saying something completely unreasonable.

"So what will you say to the police?" I asked her, my voice sharper than I intended. "That some organisation *doesn't* want to kill you?"

She opened her mouth, hesitated. "I know it sounds rubbish, but—"

Of course it did. Everything sounded rubbish lately. Kidnappings, underground fights, frozen accounts, deportation — all rubbish. But here we were, living it.

I rubbed my face, feeling the exhaustion settle into my bones. The day hadn't even properly started and I already wanted out of it.

"Let's go for a coffee," I said finally. "I haven't had my espresso today, and I feel like a zombie."

Angela

We sat over our coffees in silence.

An old man beside us, buried in his book, lifted his eyes and studied us like an exhibit.

"You two look like psychopaths," he announced. "I was complaining about youngsters glued to their phones, but you two..."

I didn't even blink.

"Do you ever watch the news?"

He smiled proudly. "I'm proud of not watching TV for the last few decades."

Robert sighed. "In other case you would know that we are two deported psychopaths."

The old man cleared his throat, turned away from us, and went back to pretending we didn't exist.

I stirred my coffee, watching the liquid spin like it was trying to escape.

"I have an idea about the last task," I said quietly. "Our shrink should know best about all our fears."

Robert

The psychotherapist stared at us in silence, the way people stare at unfamiliar insects — cautious, calculating, mildly disappointed.

Angela and I sat opposite her, waiting for something resembling professionalism.

"You two are too weird for my practice," she finally said. "I have reached my level of expertise. You need someone more advanced."

I blinked.

"Did you just call us weird?"

She tilted her head. "Do you have it recorded somewhere?"

"No."

"Well," she said, shrugging lightly, "I don't remember saying this, to be honest."

Classic. A therapist gaslighting us. Perfect.

Angela leaned forward. "To the point. We are puzzled at the moment. What is my biggest fear, and what is his biggest fear?"

The psychotherapist sighed, folded her hands, and looked at us like we were a disappointing academic project.

"Basically," she said, "you are both afraid of life."

Angela

We walked away from the therapist's office toward the bookstore. Robert was talking, trying to make sense of what we'd just heard.

"It's like a checkmate," he said. "If we're afraid of our lives, and we're supposed to face our biggest fear, then we're supposed to live life. This Coach is a smartass."

I wasn't sure if he was right, but the logic stung a little.

A van rolled up behind us, too close, too slow.

"But how is he supposed to earn his money if he doesn't want to kill us?" Robert continued to think aloud.

The door slid open.

A man jumped out.

Robert spotted him and punched him straight in the stomach.

"What the fuck? Why did you do this?" the man gasped.

Robert's fist connected with the man's face a second later. Then he yelled at me, desperate:

"Run! Run! Run!"

But I froze.

A second man popped out. They grabbed Robert and shoved him into the van. The door slammed shut.

Robert

The kidnapper sat across from me in the van, massaging the spot where my fist had landed. The second kidnapper — the one driving — reached over and slapped him in the face without even looking away from the road.

'What the hell?'

'You should be more aware of situations!'

I shifted on the floor.

'I can recommend a nice shrink for couples.' I said.

The driver glared at me through the rear-view mirror.

'Shut up! You didn't listen to us. What we've told you last time?'

'I have a short spin of memory,' I replied. 'Anyways, I don't work anymore, I also don't care for my life, so you can kill me. For free.'

They exchanged a look — the kind criminals give each other when they realise their hostage has stopped playing by the rules.

'I didn't hit him hard, it was my mild punch, I swear.' The one that hit me started to shout.

'For free? This would be a fuckin' honor to you. You don't deserve this! Get out of your clothes!' Shouted the other one to me.

I raised an eyebrow.

'Do you want to see my Big Ben again?' I asked.

One of the kidnappers started to laugh. He got immediately scolded by the other one.

'What are you laughing at? He's useless now. You damaged his head.'

Robert

They threw me out on Westminster Bridge again.

Second time this week — I was starting to feel like a piece of returning luggage.

I pulled myself together and headed straight toward the hideout where my homeless friends usually slept.

George lay curled in his nest of blankets and plastic bags, snoring softly.

I crouched beside him and touched his arm.

"Hey, it's me," I whispered.

He blinked awake, squinting at me like I'd interrupted a pleasant dream.

"Since when are you 'it's me' to me?"

"Please lend me some clothes," I said. "We need to check the mail. I've been abroad."

"Yeah, I watch the news," he muttered, digging around in his belongings. "You should be the new Diogenes, by the way."

"Pardon?"

"A philosopher from a barrel. The one who liked to walk without his clothes?"

"Right now I just need a lot of beer, I admit. But let's go, please."

"I have an appointment with my fiancée," he said with unexpected dignity, patting down his jacket.

"Just call her!"

"We are old-fashioned homeless," he replied. "No mobile phones. This is her favourite place to meet."

He said it with such seriousness that for a second I forgot how insane my own life had become.

Robert

Back in my flat, still wearing George's questionably clean clothes, I sifted through the pile of mail dumped through my door. Bills, ads, some charity begging for money I absolutely didn't have — and then a letter with the university logo.

George's name on it.

I hesitated. For a moment I even looked around the empty flat, as if anyone would catch me opening a homeless man's mail. Then I tore it open and unfolded the letter.

"For fuck's sake!" I shouted.

Robert

Marek drove fast — too fast — gripping the wheel as if the police were still after him. I sat in the backseat, clutching George's letter like it was a detonator.

"I'm so grateful that you didn't tell the police about me," Marek said, glancing at me in the mirror.

"Sorry about that," I said. "I forgot about you in all this chaos."

Marek's eyes widened. "What?!"

He almost hit a parked car.

I leaned forward.

"Just drive! We are saving someone's life!"

That shut him up.

Marek focused on the road, and I held the letter tighter, praying — for once — that I wasn't already too late.

Robert

George stood under the bridge, staring at the designer suit like it was an alien's uniform I'd dropped into his hands. I gave him the letter too. His eyes jumped from one word to the other, confused, suspicious, overwhelmed.

"You went through my post?" he asked.

"Yes," I said, "because I wanted to have a free conscience while taking a bath. You will put the suit on in the taxi. You have an appointment in thirty minutes."

He kept blinking at the suit, like it might bite him.

"What about my fiancée?"

Of course.

The man had a life full of emotional obligations, and somehow I was the one responsible for keeping them all intact.

I looked at him — this homeless philosopher with a university letter and a romantic schedule — and realised I was now managing someone else's future while my own was still on fire.

But fine.

One problem at a time.

Robert

Still wearing clothes from George, I sat under the bridge among his belongings, guarding them like some miserable dragon watching over plastic bags and two half-broken blankets.

Every few minutes I ran out to check the time, but Big Ben was still broken — of course it was — leaving me stuck.

I started stopping strangers.

"Hey man, what's the time?" I asked the first one.

"I don't have change, sorry," he said, speeding up as if homelessness was contagious.

I tried another.

"What's the time, please?"

"It's time to go to work," the second man snapped, clearly offended by my existence.

Perfect. London's finest.

I was about to ask the third when George's fiancée appeared with a dog the size of my anxiety. I jumped up immediately.

"He's OK," I said fast, "but my friend might be in trouble. She wanted to end her life, and the hitmen charity wanted to do this for her, and—"

"She is fine," the fiancée cut in calmly. "Just saw her. She used to come here quite often. You will find her on her favourite bench."

She pointed toward the river.

Of course. Angela had a favourite bench for suicidal contemplation. I should have guessed and remembered her favourite London spot.

Angela

I sat on my favourite bench, staring at the river that always looked calmer than I felt. The world moved around me like background noise — dogs, joggers, tourists taking photos of something that wasn't even beautiful.

Then Robert appeared out of nowhere and dropped onto the bench beside me, breathing hard.

"You fuckin' scared me," he said.

"Me?" I looked at him. "It's you who appeared from nowhere."

He ran a hand through his hair, still shaking a little.

"I was really afraid that you will go to the last meeting."

Before I could answer, he leaned in and hugged me. It was awkward — his jacket smelled like George's dog and adrenaline — but I didn't push him away. We sat like that, pressed together.

For a moment the city inhaled. Then Big Ben suddenly fixed itself and rang the hour like a divine punchline.

I pulled back and looked at him.

"What is it about the last meeting?"

"Whoever goes to the last meeting will be killed," he said.

My stomach dropped.

"How did I miss it? And you are telling me this now? What kind of a friend you are?"

"Don't try to friendzone me," he shot back. "You could do this a few seconds ago."

We sank into another pocket of awkward silence — two idiots with too much history and too little sense.

Then Robert exhaled and said,

"I owe you something. A revenge on Ahmed. We can arrange a nice honeymoon for him, through your friend. Is she still working there?"

Coach

My phone buzzed while I was making tea — the boring, healthy kind my wife insisted on.

A video from Angela, titled 'Revenge'.

I tapped it open, and the screen filled with chaos: a man sprinting across uneven ground, screaming, while a highlander's blond bearded man chased him with an axe raised like a patriotic flag.

I watched the whole thing twice.

A slow smile spread across my face.

They finally understood the assignment.

Bravery, chaos, unpredictability — the sort of energy normal people suppress to survive.

But not them.

I set the phone down, still smiling.

They were doing better without me than with me.

A very good sign.

However, emotions aside, I had to look at the financial side of this whole operation. I took out the Suicides Club agreements and started going through them, line by line.

Also by K. E. Adamus